Codename

Wizard

Leon Michaels

1

Books by Leon Michaels

The Path Home

From the Mists of Darkness

Task Force Nemesis

Tales From The Bench

The Echelon Factor

Today is Yesterday's Tomorrow

The Path They Have Chosen

The Morbius Expedition

Random Acts Of Science Fiction

A Rigged Deck

Willem

The Reconstruction of Cassiopeia

Post- Apocalyptic

Three Against The Darkness

"The Crane Equation Trilogy"

The Crane Equation: The Early Years

The Crane Equation: Rebuilding a Nation

The Crane Equation: The Crane Legacy

Action/Adventure

"The Black Ops Series"

Operation Damocles

Operation Dokkaebi

Operation Yofune-Nushi

Operation Kartikeya

The Black Orchid

The Twenty-First Special Operations Group: Book One: Family

ScFi-Action/Adventure

Acknowledgements

As always to my wife who reads, edits, and comments on each tale I attempt to write. She tolerates reading stories which does not interest her and gives me real time criticism needed to hopefully improve the story.

To my readers who take the chance to read my work, I offer my heartfelt thanks.

NOTE: Cover photo is a representation of the MERS Virus.

This is a work of Fiction. Any similarities to individuals past or present is unintentional and purely a coincidence. Any similarities to any individual in the future is pure Karma.

This Page Left Blank

0513 Hours, The Bunker

Lieutenant Colonel Gloria Garcia walked into the Conference Room of the Headquarters of the Twenty-First Special Operations Group to find it nearly crowded as everyone was watching the video feed from a camera attached to a rifle scope nearly half way around the world.

"Sorry I'm late. Status?" Her comments were directed to Gunnery Warrant Officer David Bricker.

"Wizard is in place. Target is moving. And we are just waiting for the game to start."

She went over to the coffee service, filled a ceramic cup with coffee and dropped a single sugar cube in the cup before going back to stand behind Gunner Bricker to watch the events they had planned for months, then waited for three weeks for everything to come together for this mission to be complete. She placed her hand on Bricker's shoulder.

"Valkyries?"

"They left the island on an Air France flight to New Zealand at 1930 hours their time. But the tropical storm approaching the island has been classified as a typhoon and Pago Pago is not allowing any inbound aircraft to land. We've got the Wizard a seat on a charter, a Gulfstream V already on the island."

"Where is it going?"

"Fiji. We have a 17 Charlie flying down from Iwakuni to pick him up, but he's going to have a bumpy flight from Samoa to Fiji."

"His cover won't protect him if the locals get to nosey and open his transport case."

The speaker in the conference room crackled with a call.

"Wizard, they are enroute, approximately five minutes."

"Understand approximately five minutes."

The call was between a deep cover CIA agent assisting the Wizard informing him the target was moving down the road where the Wizard was waiting to ambush the target.

The target was a Samoan who had spent years in the United States and had developed a Communist philosophy. Normally he would go unnoticed, but he was developing a following, preaching a philosophy which if he built enough followers, could turn the islands into a Socialist stronghold in the South Pacific.

All evidence pointed towards the target either blackmailing or paying off key government officials, preventing him from being charged with several felonies. Because of the status of America Samoa, there was nothing the American Government could do without causing major political fallout.

A chain of events led to this night on Samoa with the final determination to remove the target. Sitting in the safe in Gloria's office was a letter sanctioning this action.

In Texas, the clock seemed to creep by as they waited for the completion of the mission. In Samoa it was after eleven at night and the Wizard was experienced in waiting. On the large monitor in Texas the only actual view they had from the gun camera was the other side of the road as the Wizard was relaxed, waiting for the arrival of his target.

The Wizard was wearing polarized sunglasses instead of night vision goggles since the Toyota Land Cruiser the target would be in had to use its headlights this time of night. His goggles were on and flipped up out of the way, and if he had to

8

remove the sunglasses, they were attached to a cord, so they would only drop out of the way yet not get lost.

The monitor showed the rifle slightly shifting as the Wizard double checked to insure he was ready to fire when the target presented itself. The rifle was a non-standard M-4 carbine in that it had a fourteen-inch barrel and silencer besides being in the caliber 7.62x39, the same as the old AK-47's. His magazine held forty rounds and was also attached to a cord so when he dropped the magazine once empty, it would hang out of the way as he inserted a new magazine. The magazines were custom made and had endured over one hundred hours of testing to ensure function.

His plan was simple. He would engage the vehicle, emptying the first magazine into the windshield, killing the driver and bodyguard, then once the vehicle wrecked, go after the target and the other bodyguard. At the range he was set up for, he figured the first magazine would solve all the problems as penetration of the Chinese made 124 grain Full Metal Jacket bullets should pass through the front to the back seats. All he had to do was confirm all personal were dead before moving out of the kill zone.

"Show time." The Bunker's speakers crackled, and the monitor showed the camera moving towards the end in the road.

What the camera did not show was the faint light of the Toyota's headlights illuminating the vegetation at the bend in the road, indicating a vehicle approaching. But the Wizard's glasses picked up the light.

The lights on the vegetation became brighter then the vehicle came around the corner and in Texas, the monitor was just a glare of light. But in Samoa, the Wizard wasn't blinded by the glare of the headlights as he took aim at the vehicle approaching him. The speed limit on the Samoan Island of Tutuila was thirty miles per hour and this vehicle was exceeding that as the Wizard had predicted. At approximately seventy meters away, he opened fire on the on-rushing vehicle.

He had selected a point of aim just over the hood figuring the Full Metal Jacketed bullets would eat through the light metal under the windshield, plus any impacts into the windshield would send glass shrapnel into the interior of the vehicle. He swept from the driver's position to the left into the body guard sitting in the front seat.

When the driver was hit, he was knocked to his right and in doing so, jerked the steering wheel to the right, towards the slight drop-off at the edge of the road and crashed into the trees as bullets filled the cabin of the vehicle until the weapon's bolt locked to the rear.

The Wizard dropped the magazine as he also reached for a fresh one, slammed it into the magazine well to insure it locked up, hit the bolt release and from habit, hit the forward assist button at the rear of the receiver to insure the bolt was locked into battery. He then pulled off his sunglasses and dropped his night vision goggles down as he stepped out onto the road, and began sweeping the vehicle below the door windows, eating through the light metal and into the bodies of the humans occupying the Toyota.

When that magazine was empty, he removed it and replaced it in the pouch it came from and withdraw a third magazine as he closed on the vehicle. Mounted on the side of the forward handguard was a high intensity infrared light which he activated with the touch of his left index finger.

He did not just walk up to the vehicle, but he moved around the rear of the vehicle to the right side of the vehicle to find the doors were still closed telling him no one had dropped out during the crash. Slowly he moved to the back of the vehicle and fired three bursts through the rear window low into the back seat just in case someone there was still alive that might harm him as he then moved to the driver's side to do a final check before moving to his pick-up point.

The windows on the doors were shot out and he stepped forward and fired a long burst into the back seat before looking into the vehicle to insure his mission was complete. His target was lying across the seat with half of his head blown away. He fired a three-round burst into the body guard in the back seat then emptied the magazine into the driver and body guard in the front seats before moving away from the vehicle.

"Bunker, end of mission."

"Affirmative Wizard, we copy end of mission. We've had to change your extraction due to the developing typhon. We'll send you the information via text."

"Bunker, I copy extraction info via text. Wizard out."

In the Bunker, the video feed ended as the Wizard shut down his camera, then his communications link to the satellite high above him. Gloria addressed Gunner Bricker.

"David, package everything for Sandra's review, then go get some rest. We'll go over the mission after lunch."

"Will do Gloria."

The Wizard carefully opened the rear passenger door and jerked the target from the vehicle and smiled to himself as he saw a briefcase and computer laptop case in the floorboard. As he reached in to get them, he noticed a small, black duffle lying at the feet of the bodyguard and grabbed it also. Both the laptop case and duffle had shoulder straps, so he slung those over his left shoulder, picked up the briefcase with his left hand and took one final look around before crossing the road to his pickup point.

Twenty minutes later, the Wizard stepped out of the brush onto a road to find the CIA agent with a Ford Pick-up waiting for him. He checked the temperature of the silencer with his hand then twisted it off the end of his rifle and tossed it into the underbrush on the opposite side of the road. Reaching behind his back, he retrieved a second silencer and installed it, insuring it was tight, then just let the rifle hang from its single-point sling as he walked to the truck.

"How did it go?" He was asked by the agent.

"Felix, unless Solaita has a twin, he will no longer be a problem."

"Fair enough."

The Wizard handed the briefcase and the laptop to Felix.

"You know what to do with those."

"Yeah, let me open the computer and pull the hard drive for you while you get cleaned up. What's in the duffle?"

"I was just going to check it out."

When he opened the duffle, even the red lens of his pen light could not hide the contents. It was full of money. Actually, bundles of United States $100.00 bills. He pulled two bundles out and laid them aside, then set the duffle aside for the moment as he had other things to do.

The Wizard opened the shipping container in the back of the truck and removed the packing tray, so he could put his gear in the bottom. The rifle was broken down into two pieces then slipped into special paper sleeves designed to prohibit rust as he knew it could be days before he would have time to properly clean the rifle before it goes back into storage.

He began layering the rest of the money from the duffle in on top of his other gear and waited until Felix had the hard drive out and placed in a protective anti-static bag for transport. Felix then quickly went through the briefcase, sorting out what he was going to keep for his operation on the island and putting the rest in a large, sealable plastic bag.

When he handed the Wizard the drive and documents, he received the two bundles of money the Wizard had set aside.

"Here ya go Felix, overtime pay."
"This from the duffle?"

"Yeah. If they bundled that right, you have about twenty thousand there. Be smart and do not get carried away with it otherwise someone might notice and put a bullet in your brain. Understand?"

"Yeah, I understand, but is this legal? I mean you giving me this cash?"

"Listen, the folks I work for won't even ask if there was any money handy and if I turn over the rest of it, they'll never ask if I kept any. They're funny like that. So, keep your mouth shut and enjoy it in very small portions."

"You got it. Finish up, we need to get moving."

The clothing he was wearing was non-descript meaning he could wear them back to his room before showering and changing to leave the island. He took time to clean the make-up off his face intended to hide his features before closing the case, then placing tape seals on it showing it had gone through a customs check to prevent any inquisitive customs agent from looking into it. He had to chuckle at the thought of some agent wanting to look inside the case with its radioactive labels all over the case.

It was nearly an hour before he walked into his room, stripped and entered the shower. After double checking his bags, he laid down for a few hours sleep before Felix was to pick him up to take him to the airport.

Pago Pago International Airport

Dolores Ramone was an up and coming Mexican-American actress and at the age of twenty-six had her first major motion picture climbing up the Billboard money tree and she had just finished an Asian tour supporting the opening of the movie. She took some time off to visit American Samoa because she had heard about the quiet sandy beaches. Currently she was sitting in a Gulfstream V waiting for it to take her to Fiji and another beach before heading back to the states. The pilot informed her and the other passengers that were at a hold until the last passenger arrived. Looking out her window she watched as a Ford pickup drove up to the plane and deposited another passenger for the plane.

He took several hard cases out of the back of the truck and put them into the cargo hold under the passenger compartment before boarding with a medium size nylon duffle. She had noticed the cases were marked USGS which she remembered as being United States Geological Society. He took a seat in front facing her and buckled himself in without saying a word to anyone. She figured he was about six foot two, two hundred plus but his build was solid. He was deeply tanned with close cropped hair with a mustache and needing a shave.

The Wizard took in his traveling companions without the obvious staring. There was a couple, most likely American tourists one row back on either side of the narrow aisle. To his right, a businessman, most likely European and from his clothing possibly a Frenchman. In from of him was an attractive female, mid-twenties, nice body hidden under loose clothing and from her complexion and facial features, most likely Mexican.

When he stretched out after laying his seat back a bit after they took off, she took him in even more. He was wearing a tan polo shirt that fit him snuggly without being over tight and tan khaki trousers with cargo pockets that appeared to be empty. He was wearing matching boots that were clean yet worn, and he had a chain around his neck, but it was tucked into his shirt hiding

15

whatever was dangling from it and his wristwatch was expensive yet unlike most men wearing gold or silver watches, this one was a muted black. Dolores considered him ruggedly handsome but not a man she would pay a lot of attention to back in Hollywood.

They were nearly two hours into the flight when he sudden sat up and cocked his head as if he was listening to something. He raised his seat back up and pulled his seatbelt tight then loudly yelled "fasten your seatbelts." Dolores looked at him as if he had lost his mind then she felt a tremor in the airplane and as she was reaching for her own seatbelts there was an explosion behind her and the plane nearly became upside down in flight. She was thrown out of her seat forward and as she was basically flying past the man he reached out and grabbed her then pulled her onto his lap wrapping his arms around her to keep her from further movement.

For the first couple of seconds it felt as if he was going to squeeze the air out of her then he shifted his grip slightly and she could breath. Somewhere in the seconds from him grabbing her to the plane stabilizing she realized he was crushing her left breast with his hand as he held onto her. When the plane had stabilized for several seconds, he almost threw her back into her seat telling her to buckle up. She landed awkwardly, but straightened herself and once more grabbed her seatbelts.

He unfastened his and was moving to the rear of the plane. Dolores looked over her shoulder and two of the passengers were on the floor. There were only five passengers on this flight and she looked to the fifth to see him in his seat gripping the armrests just staring straight ahead. She looked forward and saw the first aid kit hanging on the cockpit wall and figured the man might need it. He was carefully moving the female and when he got her on her back, there was a gash in her head bleeding profusely. He started to rise and Dolores was there with the kit holding it out to him. He told her thanks in Spanish and went to work on the woman. It did not take him long to press a gauze compress on her then wrapped her head with gauze to keep it in place. He quickly checked her body looking for broken bones before gently lifting her back into her seat. He got her strapped in and told Dolores to hold her head up and against the seats headrest. Using more gauze, he wrapped her head to the headrest. It took a couple seconds digging through the kit to come up with a small penlight. He tested it to insure it worked then checked the woman's eyes. He told Dolores to hold her as he moved back into the plane and retrieved his duffle. From it he took two web belts that she recognized a rigger's belts from when she wore one in a cheap Sci-Fi movie when she was just getting into the business. He wrapped the belts around the unconscious woman and the seat at chest level holding her upright.

The other passenger had gotten himself back into his chair but was holding his arm. When they moved to him he told them he thought it was broken and a quick exam confirmed that. His arm was put into a sling and when he asked how his wife was he was told she had a gash on her forehead and had suffered a concussion. Dolores went back to her seat and strapped in as the plane shuddered. Her savior moved back to his seat with his duffle and once more strapped in. He looked at her and nodded thanks to her and she responded with a weak smile.

Dolores felt her ears pop telling her they were losing altitude and the fear she already had streaming through her body was intensified. She looked at the man in front of her and he was just sitting there with his head against the headrest with his eyes closed as if nothing was happening, except there was blood on his clothing and hands from rendering first aid to the woman behind her. The passenger compartment speaker crackled then the pilot spoke.

"Folks we just had a catastrophic failure of the starboard engine. It exploded causing damage to our tail section and we are losing altitude. We are too far from any safe landing fields but we are within range of some deserted islands. We are going to try to make a water landing putting ourselves close enough to shore to minimize the risk of you getting to shore and safety. One major problem is that area is receiving rain, a tropical thunderstorm, but it is our only option at this time. We are sending out a May Day but have yet to receive any reply on the International Distress Frequency. We will let you know when we are about to splash down so you can brace yourselves. Good Luck, and I am really sorry about this."

Dolores watched as he leaned over to his duffle and began to take things from it and shove into his cargo pants pockets. Around his right leg he strapped on a large knife from his knee down to his ankle. Once finished he just sat back down and acted as if this was a daily occurrence for him. She looked at him and wondered how he could remain so calm when death was inches away. The aircraft was being buffeted by the storm and she could see rain hitting the window beside her seat. He got up, opened his bag and took a long strap out of it and a small pouch then went back to the man with the broken arm.

He put the strap around the man's chest holding him into the chair and his arm tight against his body. He took a bright orange knife from the pouch and using the lanyard attached to it put it on the man's good wrist. He showed him how to use the knife and she realized it was an oddly built switchblade that instead of a blade a hook popped out of it. He injured man smiled and then her man went to the scared man across the aisle and talked to him for a minute. He returned to his seat and looked at her for a second then spoke to her in flawless Spanish.

"When it is time to land, follow my actions. It will help take the impact of a hard landing."

His voice was strong and deep.

She replied back in Spanish. "Thank you I will and I'm a Tex-Mex."

He smiled and in English spoke again. "One never can be sure these days."

When the speaker told them to prepare themselves, he bent over and wrapped both arms around his legs. Dolores did the same and was glad she had worn slacks instead of a dress as she originally intended to do. The man across the aisle did the same and they waited for the end of their flight.

The cockpit crew was doing everything they could to bring the aircraft down safely, but it was hard to read the water with the waves under them reacting to the storm and the rain interfering with reading the distance to the island they were approaching. The pilot dumped the fuel tanks and they had decided that with the vertical stabilizer damaged it was too risky to reverse the remaining engine to reduce their airspeed. They did everything they could to bleed off the airspeed but both knew that the aircraft was going to end up on the beach if they were lucky, and well into the jungle growth if not. The plane skipped twice on the waves as they fought to hold the nose up and then it skimmed across the surface of the water then up onto the beach.

Dolores heard a horrible noise from the cockpit like metal being ripped apart and a man's voice screaming for just a second. The man was reacting even before the plane stopped shuddering, going back to the injured man and woman. He got the man free and then the woman. No one had come out of the cockpit yet but the man across the aisle from her was working to get the door open. Her man had the injured woman in his arms and was moving to the door when the other man got it open. Rain was pouring in and the other man took the emergency light from the wall and shined it out onto the ground, then sat down on the edge of the door and jumped to the ground.

Her man told her to get out and help when he passed the injured out the door. She did as she was told and moments later the woman was passed through the door and then her husband. Her man moved to the cockpit and kicked the door in so he could enter. Minutes later he passed the co-pilot out the door. The next time she saw him he was passing luggage out the door that was in the cabin then the first aid kits. Tools that were stored in the cabin and then a plastic trash bag full of whatever he had collected. He jumped out then went to work on the steps tucked away under the door frame and got them down so they could use them to go back into the craft. As he was getting that rigged she asked him about the pilot. His only reply was dead.

He took the large emergency light from the other man, then took them away from the aircraft and into the jungle. They were soaked and the rain seemed to be getting worse. He took the emergency tools back to the plane and began to open the cargo compartments pulling luggage and his boxes from it. The other man helped drag the luggage to their location as the injured man just held his wife the best he could. Dolores went to help and found his cases were heavier then she could handle but still drug one to their spot. She watched him move with precision with no waste of energy or movement. He found a plastic tarp in the cargo hold and stretched it out and just laid it over the rest of them the best he could to give them some protection from the rain. The co-pilot finally came too and tried to help but he was hurting from the force of impact against his straps.

Her man broke the custom seals on one of his cases and opened it removing a military looking vest and from it he took an odd-looking phone from it. He raised the antenna on it and looked at the small screen for a minute then began to punch up his menu.

In Texas the Duty Officer saw the encrypted data on his computer monitor telling him it was Joshua Kramer calling in.

"Go ahead Wizard."

"Connect me with the Orchid."

Gloria was in her quarters, watching television with her son Marco when the phone on the living room desk began to ring. Her movements were quick without bothering her son's attention to the Disney movie they were watching.

20

"Orchid here, who is this?"

"Orchid, this is Kramer, my plane went down during this storm. I have one dead, three injured and myself and two others uninjured. The pilots put us on a deserted island from what I know at this time."

"Understand, I'm transferring you back to the Duty Officer, give him your GPS and all the information possible. Take care, we'll see what we can do to get you off that island as quickly as possible."

"Will do Orchid."

"Major Mattson break this down and assist the Wizard."

The Duty Officer at the Bunker always listened to the conversations coming in from operators and was ready to do his end of the business. He had already signaled the Bunker's night crew that they had an operator in trouble when he heard about the plane crash over the phone.

Delores watched as he spoke into the phone, but she could not hear what he was saying. He put the phone down and got back into the case removing another item which he turned on then sat down in front of him before picking the phone back up. He spoke for about a minute then turned the phone back off. He sat there for a few minutes as if catching his breath then opened the large case and removed a machete from it and went to work constructing them a shelter.

Delores and the other man walked up to him as he was lashing a pole to a tree with thin vines.

"What can we do to help?" She asked him.

He took the orange knife from his pocket then the large knife from his leg scabbard and told them to cut the carpet out of the aircraft. It was only held down along the edge and around the seats. Do not get fancy just rip it out and they could use it as best it would fit to cover the frame once it is finished.

"My name is Delores. Yours?"

"Joshua, Joshua Kramer."

The other man introduced himself as Phillip and he had a strong French accent. They went to work on the carpet ripping it out while Joshua built the frame. It took nearly three hours to get the shelter up and move everyone into it out of the rain. Joshua leaned against one of the support trees looking like a drowned rat and she could tell he was becoming exhausted from his labors for them. She herself was fighting off sleep and Phillip was laid out snoring. She moved to Joshua.

"What more can we do?"

"Go back to the plane and strip it of everything that can catch water. Then get anything that you every think might be useful even if at the moment you can find no use for it."

She woke Phillip up and they went back to the plane. Joshua checked on the injured. The woman's eyes were reacting better than when he first checked her out but she was still unconscious. With the co-pilots help, Joshua set the broken arm the best he could and splinted it. He checked the co-pilot and determined he had cracked ribs and bound him up the best he could from the first aid kits. Dolores and Phillip began to bring trash bags back with all sorts of times in them. Phillip returned one time with two cases of bottled water they found in a cabinet. Joshua drank a full bottle of water without taking it from his mouth.

The co-pilot told Phillip where to look in the cockpit for emergency items. Philip returned with some but said he could not get to the others because of the pilots body. Joshua took a small folding saw from his box and went with Phillip telling Dolores to stay behind in the shelter. A large tree limb had been driven through the wind screen on the cockpit and entered the pilot's chest pinning him to the seat as it killed him. Joshua cut the limb and they got the pilot out of the cockpit and laid out on the floor of the cabin. They gathered up the rest of the supplies and left the aircraft as the tide began to move in and the tail section was being floated off the beach.

When they got back to the shelter, Dolores sat and watched him as he once more used his odd telephone and made a call. He talked on it a few minutes before shutting it back down and then looked at everyone in the shelter.

"Good news, the U.S. Navy has our location and they're sending a Frigate our way to pick us up. Bad news is we are on the eastern edge of a typhoon and it may be as long as four days before they get here. The tide is coming in and there is a possibility it will float the aircraft off the beach so come daylight let's take one last go at getting everything off it we can. Another thing is this island has not been survived for nearly thirty years so there is no current information other that there were feral hogs on it then. I'll try to get us some meat after daylight if there are any still on the island. For now, get your rest."

Dolores had brought all the small airline bottles of whiskey and such off the plane and she opened two bottles of Jack Daniels pouring them into one of the aircrafts plastic coffee cups.

"Here Joshua, drink this. We'll keep watch while you get some rest."

He looked at the cup then took it and drank it all down in one long swallow. He handed her the cup back then opened his large case taking out two odd looking paper sleeves. Dolores recognized what he pulled from them and assembled. It was an M-16 style rifle with holographic sights. He checked the sights then pulled a magazine from the case, checked it and inserted it into the rifle and chambered a round. Joshua shifted and leaned back against the tree supporting the shelter's frame and laid the rifle across his lap.

"Joshua, who the hell are you?" She asked.

"I'm a First Lieutenant in the Marine Corps." And with that he closed his eyes and within minutes was softly snoring.

Dolores fought sleep for two hours then woke Phillip and then she went to sleep. She was awakened by Phillip as he shook her shoulder. She could tell it was daylight even with the pounding rain but Joshua was not under the shelter. She looked at her watch and saw that she had been asleep for five hours.

"Where is Joshua?"

"I do not know. I fell asleep and he was gone when I woke up a few minutes ago. I am sorry but I was very tired."

"Don't worry we are all tired, and he seems more than capable of taking care of himself. Get some rest, we may have more things to do when he returns."

It was nearly an hour before she saw him step out of the jungle in front of the shelter. He had change his clothing as was now wearing a Camouflage uniform and floppy hat along with his vest that had a pistol in a holster in the front of it. His rifle was hanging across his body and in his left hand he had a small pig that appeared to have already been gutted. He dropped the pig in front of the shelter and stepped in out of the rain.

"Well if I can get a fire going, we have lunch."

By this time everyone to include the injured woman was awake. She was sitting up next to her husband who was holding her against him with his good arm. Joshua told Dolores what to look for as far as wood was concerned and she and Phillip went looking for wood along the beach. He told them not to venture

24

into the jungle because of the hogs and what else might lie in wait to do them harm. They brought back wood that he split then split again using his machete to expose the dry insides. She watched him start a small fire under the shelter utilizing a jell from a tube he took from his case, then carefully moved it out to the edge of the rain and added wood to build it up.

He took some time to stretch a military poncho across the shelter dividing it, so they could change into some dry clothes in private. She helped the injured woman change then the men used it. Dolores admitted it felt good to get into dryer clothes even though most were damp. During his time raiding the airplane, Joshua had taken a long, steel crank rod from the cargo bay and when he was happy with the fire he skinned then ran the rod through the carcass. He found two 'Y' shaped limps which he stuck in the ground and hung the pig over the fire roasting it. Dolores had taken a couple of salt containers from the plane and he salted the carcass to add flavor to it.

Joshua spent some time building another shelter just feet away from the main one and enclosed the side with the opening away from them. He told them if they had to use the restroom there it was, just try to hit the hole he had scraped out of the sandy soil.

The fire put heat into the shelter and soon the dampness was gone from their clothing. He had stripped down to his t-shirt and had hug his top and vest up to dry. He also used the time to clean and oil his rifle and double check his pistol before adding some more wood to the fire and once more leaning back against his tree. He told Dolores to keep the fire about that height and to turn the pig every few minutes then wake him in two hours.

She woke him on time and he checked the meat pronouncing it would be another hour. He told her to put out the things she gathered up to collect water in so they could save as much of the bottled water as possible.

Joshua got back on the phone and was told the weather over his location was going to break sometime before dark but the rescue vessel was still fighting the storm and their arrival was still as first determined. He updated his contact on the status on the injured passengers and then closed the contact. Joshua briefed everyone how things were going and then put his hat on and walked towards the beach with his rifle. He returned about forty five minutes later with a rusted tin can with water in it and sat it on the fire to boil the water. Dolores watched and wondered what he was doing. They ate pork until everyone was full and drank rain water. It wasn't the best meal but the meat was hot and the water cool. Everyone ate their fill and just relaxed to wait out their rescue.

Dolores went to the toilet after taking a pair of shorts out of her bag and put them on instead of her pants. She pulled her blouse off in the shelter and told Joshua she was going to try to gather more wood along the beach. Her bra was concealing but did enhance her breasts and the shorts were showing a lot of leg. Her stomach was not firm but it was also not fleshy. Joshua admired the view but tried not to seem to stare at her. Phillip went with her and in about an hour they had a nice stack of wood handy at the shelter. Dolores had a beach towel in her bag and dried off then put a pull over shirt on. Just before dark she changed back into her pants as the rain slackened. By midnight there were stars in the sky.

The days were always the same. Joshua would slip off into the jungle to return later with a small pig to eat. Phillip had watched him split the wood and took that detail over with Dolores doing what she could to help the injured. She never looked in the can he had put on the fire but it seemed he used it several times during their stay. On the morning of the fourth day he dumped the contents out and she saw a half dozen long ivory tusks. She looked at Joshua who smiled at her.

"Momma hog does not appreciate her babies being killed for food. I had to kill the big ones to get to the little ones. These are their tusks."

He handed her one that was clean of all meat and flesh. She looked at it and realized these could rip a person apart real fast. He had been going out at great risk to feed them.

At midday on the fourth day he started a fire on the beach and once it was going strong he began to add green material causing it to smoke. He continued to build the fire until it was a large blazing pile while adding the green material. Within an hour a Navy helicopter over flew the beach signaling them. Joshua pointed out to sea and after a few seconds Dolores saw the frigate moving towards them from over the horizon.

In just over an hour the frigate came as close to the island as it safely could and launched a Zodiac boat. The boat took everyone except Joshua back to the frigate and as they were unloading four sailors got into the boat and it went back to the island. When it returned they had the pilot in a body bag and all of their bags. Dolores had resisted going below decks to the ships medical bay until she saw Joshua step onto the ship's deck, salute the flag at the rear of the ship, then salute the officer that was supervising the deck operations.

On the way back to Samoa, they met an aircraft carrier and Joshua was transferred to it via helicopter with all his gear. Dolores had seen little of him during their time on the frigate and hated to see him leave. He had stopped by the medical bay where they were all being kept too say goodbye, but it was just for a minute and then he was gone.

When they got to Samoa they were met by several Navy officers who as a group briefed them that under no circumstances were they to mention Joshua's presence on the crashed aircraft. They all said if it was not for him, no telling if they would have survived the first night. They wrote statements confirming his response to the crash and what he had done of the island, and then they signed non-disclosure agreements concerning his presence with them. Three days later Dolores was sitting in her condo in Pasadena wondering if he had found her card.

Joshua was going through his gear reorganizing his cases and cleaning his weapons when he found a card in his vest. It was soaked, but readable. It was the personal card for Dolores Ramone with her phone number on it. He laid it out to dry and smiled at the thought of her in just her bra and shorts.

Two days later he was on a Navy COD (Carrier On-board Delivery aircraft), heading to Pearl Harbor and a long debriefing by two members of the Twenty-First Special Operations Group. When he opened his case and showed the money, the Marine Gunny handling the debriefing just leaned over, closed the case and smiled. It was over a week later that he stepped off a C-17 at Camp Pendleton and taken to his parent unit, the First Force Recon Battalion.

After he had all his gear stowed and the money stashed away, he sat in his quarters and looked at the card. He had seen some news articles about Dolores having survived the crash and figured why not, and called her. When he got her answering machine, he left only his name and his cell phone number. Later he read an internet news article about the crash and that all of the survivors hinted to one of the men taking charge and keeping them safe without any specifics. Two nights later he saw Dolores on the talk show out of New York and realized why he got her answering machine.

One thing he noticed that as she sat talking to the host she had something in her hand. When the host asked about it she showed him the tusk he had given her, and she explained how she had gotten it without mentioning his name. He looked at some of the photos on the web of her after she returned and it seemed she had the tusk with her everywhere she went.

Three days later his phone rang.

"Joshua?"

"Hi Dolores, how are you doing?"

"Fine. Do you know a couple of producers want to make a movie of our surviving the crash and want me to play myself in it?"

"Well, I saw your new movie last night. You'll be great in the part. Just play yourself."

She laughed. "Joshua, thank you for everything you did for us."

"Dolores, it was just something that had to be done, and I just happened to be there to do it."

"That's very modest of you, but it is sad that you will never receive the praise you deserve."

"Dolores, I do not do what I do for praise. It's just a job that has to be done. What I did was for myself as much as for the group. So let's leave it at that and find another topic to discuss."

"Are you married?"

"No, and I have no girlfriend either in case you are wondering."

There was a long silence from her end so he made the move.

"Dolores say what you are thinking."

"Joshua, would you like to come up to Pasadena and have dinner with me sometime?"

29

"Tex-Mex?"

She laughed. "Sure, but no pork. I think I have had enough pork for a while."

"Well, I can't argue with that. Dolores I know you have an odd schedule in your business, but I start thirty days leave on Monday. So you pick the day and I'll be there."

"Let me call you back after I talk to my agent. He is trying to run my legs off with publicity appearances with the crash."

"I'll be expecting your call, but if I do not answer just leave the message or text me. I have a few things I have to do until Monday."

"Alright, bye Joshua and be careful."

"Bye Dolores."

On Friday he received a text from Dolores saying Monday was fine and had her address attached along with what time. Dolores spent the weekend cleaning her condo and shopping for dinner. She was nervous about the dinner and when she thought about it she could not come up with an answer why. She had a nice sun dress laid out on her bed and she worked at the dinner until she barely had time to shower then dress. She kept everything simple even avoiding perfume and makeup. After all, he had seen at her worst.

Joshua rang her doorbell a minute before the time suggested. When she opened it he was dressed in slacks, a collared shirt and sports jacket. He presented her with a bottle of white wine and she invited him in. She had everything warming and put the fajita meat on as he opened the wine. Fifteen minutes later he held her chair as she sat down at her table and he took the chair opposite her. Dinner was pleasant and she told him about the non-disclosure agreement. His tone at that point was stern, yet not disagreeable in that the subject of his disappearance was not to be discussed.

"Dolores, leave that subject alone. I cannot discuss that no more than you can. I am really enjoying this time with you but I will leave if you continue down this avenue. And I would really like to stay."

"I'm sorry Joshua, I guess we shall have to pretend we have just met."

"Yes, please follow that concept."

She looked at him and nodded her head. The subject did cover her castaway friends in that everyone was healing up nicely and Phillip had even contacted her about having dinner some time when he was in the country. She told Joshua that if he brought his wife she would go out to dinner with them, but not alone. It seems he was drooling all the time they were gathering wood when she was only wearing her bra. Joshua laughed at that then told her he also drooled a bit seeing her in that bra. Dolores actually blushed and continued to eat dinner.

After dinner they sat out on her balcony watching the sun sit and sipped on the wine. She asked him if there was anything he could tell her about what he did in the Marines, and he just told her he had command of a platoon of infantry and would probably have to leave them for a staff job soon. When asked about her career, she told him she had two television shows to do soon, and a movie starting in four months. She asked him if he had any plans for his leave and he told her that he had none. She reached over and took his hand.

"Then stay with me if you do not have any place to be."

"Dolores, we barely know each other."

"True, but what we do know about each other is something no two people will ever know. And those that do know may not survive the experience."

"Well we certainly survived."

Dolores got up from her chair, straddled him, then kissed him hard and for a long time.

"God Joshua, I have wanted to do that since the second night we were on the beach."

She looked at him then got off and walked just inside her condo. He rose out of his chair and watched her as she walked into the condo dropping her sun dress to the floor and walked through the house. She was only wearing a pair of red short boy panties and he smiled, then followed her into the condo closing the French doors behind him. She stopped at her bedroom door and turned to look at him.

"Joshua, I'm not one to just jump in bed with a man, especially without several dates beforehand. But we spent three nights together in conditions unlike any date could possibly duplicate. I'm no whore and will not be treated as one, but tonight I want to act like one with you if you wish. You are not the most attractive man I have ever dated, but you are more man than all of them put together."

"Dolores, we do not have to do this, and before you get upset, you are a very desirable woman. Also I could never think of you as being a whore. I did not come here tonight with visions of your naked body next to mine, but to know you without the tension of surviving a crashed airplane hanging over us."

"Are you turning me down?"

He looked at her for a long time admiring her body and her hard nipples pushing away from her breasts.

"I must be out of my mind but yes, I am turning you down tonight."

Dolores started laughing then walked up to him, pulled his face down to hers and kissed him. He wrapped his arms around her and felt her hot skin in his hands. She broke the kiss and pushed away from him. She laughed again as she walked around him and picked up her dress. She spoke as she was putting the dress back on.

"If any man but you had just done that I would be real upset, and probably throwing things at him as he scurried out the door, but for some odd reason I can't be mad at you. We slept together for three nights without ever touching or seeing one another naked. Now you know exactly what I look like except for my pubic. So tonight you are going to take me out for a drink or two, and we will just talk. Then you can sleep in my spare bedroom tonight. Tomorrow let's see where things lead."

He looked at her, shook his head before speaking.

"Delores, we can't go out. You can't be seen with me in public for the very reasons we cannot talk about what I was doing on that airplane. I'm going to violate a bit of security here, but if the wrong people see us together and start putting two and two together, your life could be at risk as would at least one other individual, maybe even the other passengers. I can't be more explicate than that."

Dolores looked at him for a moment and could see in his eyes his concern for her and others.

"I'm sorry Josh, I should have known from the way we were briefed about the crash. So, what do we do now?"

"We can do what we never had a chance to do on the island. We can talk, or maybe watch a movie on tv?"

They did both as they watched a goofy ScFi movie on COMET until nearly eleven. She stood and once more she stripped to her panties before offering her hand to him and escorted him to the spare bedroom.

"Joshua, I will be sleeping in the nude and you are required to do the same."

She pushed his jacket off his shoulders and then unbuttoned his shirt. When his chest was bare she ran her hand over it noticing the scars it bore then pushed herself as close as her breasts would allow and kissed him goodnight. She walked out of the room stopping at the door and took her panties off never turning to show him her pubic and tossed her panties over her shoulder at him. They were both laughing as she entered her bedroom and he got undressed for bed.

When Joshua rolled over to get out of bed, Dolores was standing in his door completely nude. He looked at her then shook his head before getting out of bed. Joshua had followed her instructions and was also naked. She giggled when he stood, walked into the bathroom and took a piss without closing the door. He came back to the bed, picked up his boxer shorts and put them on then walked up to her and kissed her hard while grabbing her ass and squeezing both buttocks hard. She gasped under his kiss and shivered from his hands on her. He broke the kiss, slapped her on her ass and told her to put some panties on. She yelped at the sting his hand produced on her ass and was laughing as she was rubbing her ass while going to her room. She returned a few minutes later wearing only a powder blue pair of short boy panties.

"Well, you said panties; you did not say a thing about any other clothes."

After breakfast, he told her to shower and dress casual but hide the important parts. First, they drove down to Camp Pendleton where he packed a bag telling her it would do for a week. From there they went to the VA Hospital at Long Beach where he told her they were going to visit a friend. At the hospital she met an older man missing both legs and an arm who he kept calling Gunny. They spent almost an hour with him before leaving. In the car she silently cried over what she had seen. He took her hand and held it for a time not saying a word.

"Why did you take me to see him?"

"Because that is my world Dolores. That is one of the toughest Marines I have ever known and he still paid a high price for what we do. I can leave for parts unknown and come home like that or not at all. I just wanted you to know that before we get too far into this experiment we are into."

"I should hate you for doing that to me, but I can't. Please take me home."

Dolores barely spoke during the drive home and at her condo she just went to her room as Josh went to his and began putting his things in the spare bedroom's dresser. Minutes later she walked into his room, naked as the day she was born and walked up to him, pulled his head down and kissed him with a passion he had not felt from her since he first walked into her home.

"Josh, enough of these games, take me to bed and make love to me."

He put the rest of his things on top of the dresser, stripped the bed covers off and as he was removing his clothes, she crawled onto the bed and waited for him.

Mecca

As Josh and Dolores were tearing her sheets up, events were taking place in Saudi Arabia which would affect the entire world.

Six dark men were rigging up two long pipes, extending thirty feet into the air above a five ton Mercedes truck. The pipes were connected to a two hundred liter tank containing a virulent strain of the MERS virus in a sterilized water solution. The purpose of the pipes was to atomize the base liquid and get the virus as high as possible into the air so the light, night breeze would carry it towards Mecca and the tent city of nearly a million pilgrims who had came to perform their Hajj, their pilgrimage to Mecca.

The MERS virus in its normal form was known to killed three to four individuals out of every ten exposed to it, but this strained was potent and the tests on it showed it should kill upwards of seventy percent in tests its designers had conducted.

Two hundred meters from the truck, three Saudi Army personnel lay in a ditch with bullets in their brains. They were part of the security detail who had the night shift guarding the pilgrims from harm.

Once the pipes were installed and braced, a muffled generator was started then an air compressor began pressuring the tank. When the pressure reached the calculated pressure inside the tank, valves opened to the pipes and contents began to spew from the specially constructed ends, atomizing the liquid into the atmosphere.

After double checking the gauges twice, the leader of the group brought the people together and each man drew an auto-injector from his uniform leg pouch and injected themselves with what they were told was the antidote for the virus. Each man held up his injector, so the others could see it had been activated.

Five minutes later the last man gasped for air as he died from a neural toxin he had injected into his body. Three hundred meters away, this was witnessed by another man through night vision binoculars who just smiled before walking to his Ranger Rover and driving back to Riyadh, and the blond prostitute he had waiting for him there.

The pressure valves on the trucks equipment would register the difference between the air pressure pushing the liquid from the tank and just air flowing through it once the tank was empty. At that point, a timer would take over and two minutes later cause the generator to shut down, shutting the rest of the system down.

It had been proposed that a destructive charge be set to destroy the tank and such, but that would also warn the Saudi's of the situation before the virus had a chance to spread properly.

The night breeze and the terrain spread the virus into a wider span, called the Down Wind Vapor Hazard diagram, covering over two-thirds of the encampment, plus Mecca itself. Those not immediately infected with the virus, would contact it from being on the tents and walking surfaces until the sun was high enough and its ultra-violet radiation began to deteriorate the virus.

It would be almost two hours before the word went out to find the missing security patrol, then another hour before a search helicopter was launched to assist in the search. There was no moon this night and the helicopter found the five ton truck using Forward Looking Infrared. When they saw the bodies cooling next to the truck, they landed to see what was happening and became exposed to the MERS virus.

It was nearly daylight before a full team of officers arrived at the site to begin their investigation and none of the men were wearing protective equipment at that time. They also became infected. It would be near mid-morning that someone finally woke up to the fact they had a major problem developing as the helicopter crew had returned to its base and the crew were spreading the virus amongst the people they came in contact with. Some of those people were US Military personnel stationed at Riyadh as part of the US presence in the Gulf Region.

But the biggest problem was that several plane loads of pilgrims had already left that morning to return home in Europe, Asia, and the United States. Those planes that were able too were turned around to return to Saudi Arabia, while the others were to be quarantined at the nearest airport until final determination of the seriousness of the spread of the virus could be determined.

As word was going out to the World Health Organization (WHO), others were being notified as Saudi doctors were finally able to identify the problem as those still in the tent city were slowly showing signs of the virus. Mecca itself was inspected and closed as it was thoroughly covered with the virus.

In the United States, the Center for Disease Control were packing up specialized vehicles for shipment with scientists to assist in this situation. By the end of the day, the situation became worse as the older pilgrims and infants were becoming ill at an alarming rate.

The bodies found at the truck proved to be a problem as it was found that all of their fingerprints had been removed by acid and one individual showed signs of cosmetic surgery on his face. Interpol was contacted to see if they could provide support in discovering who these men were, and where they were from.

In the Twenty-First Special Operations Group Headquarters, the intelligence personnel were working overtime sorting through the volumes of emails and phone conversations they had hacked into to see if they could get a handle on what was happening half-way around the world.

Lieutenant Colonel Garcia was standing in the conference room watching the information coming in on the Eighty-four inch television set up as a computer monitor and divided into six separate screens.

Brigadier General Sandra Grainger walked into the room and stood slightly behind Garcia, looking at the data being posted to the monitor.

"Gloria, what do you think?" Sandra asked.

"Sandra, I think the Saudi's have a catastrophe on their hands and the loose ends are on fire."

"We have any teams in the area?"

"No, from the estimate of the Down Wind Vapor Hazard predictions, our people in Iraq are safe, but I've ordered them to shift locations if possible until their missions are complete, then home PDQ."

"How'd the Saudi's identify the bug?" Sandra asked.

"They're use to battling the MERS virus, but from the report they sent to WHO and the CDC, this strain appears to be more virulent than normal. Whomever set this up seems to have given the virus a booster shot."

Sandra moved closer to the monitor and using the touch screen expanded one monitor to get a better look at the casualty figure report as of twenty minutes ago.

"My God are these figures correct?"

"Yes Ma'am. We have them directly from the Saudi's as they are reporting them to WHO." Replied Air Force Master Sergeant Karen Watkins, the number two in Electronic Intelligence.

"If I read this right, there could be upwards of one hundred thousand deaths within forty-eight hours in the Mecca area alone." Sandra commented.

"I think it'll go higher, Sandra." Gloria commented. "And it has spread to Riyadh. We also have American Air Force personnel reporting in sick after contact with a Saudi helicopter crew that found the vehicle and the dead individuals that initiated this calamity."

Sandra looked at the photos of the dead men found at the truck.

"Anything on those men yet?"

"No, but the Saudi's have sent DNA samples to Tel Aviv University since they have the best labs in the region to run the samples. Hopefully it'll give the intelligence people to work with." Gloria commented. "But whoever set this up has to have some very elaborate laboratory facilities. Next question is how they were able to get the equipment into the country."

The days for the staff of the Twenty-First was long as they were sorting through volumes of data being sent back and forth between countries, often seeing things one country or another may not see due to political reasons.

In California, Josh and Delores were just passing time, learning about each other in and out of bed when she was not attending script meetings or doing interviews about her movie, surviving the crash, and any other tidbit of trivia the show's host came up with.

Eight days after the attack, the Saudi Government released the death tolls up to that time. Three hundred twenty-seven thousand, six hundred and ninety-three deaths as of twelve o'clock, local time. The Saudi's announced they were going to cremate the bodies since they had no manner to store the dead and the virus was still active in the bodies. This upset several Islamic groups who proclaimed the victims would not receive a proper burial. The WHO reinforced the decision, as did the CDC and the governments of half the European countries where the virus was starting to make an appearance.

Before the results of the attackers DNA were released by Tel Aviv, they suggested other labs be provided with samples of the DNA since there was a rumbling of discontent by a few of the more radical Muslim countries that the Israeli's might skew the data if it might point in their direction. Samples were sent to John Hopkins in the U.S., Zurich University Hospital in Switzerland, and Tokyo University of Science in Japan.

As the other labs were processing the samples, the Israeli Mossad sent the results from Tel Aviv to the Twenty-First SOG since they had long since learned the Twenty-First found answers to problems no one else seemed to discover. The secret of the Twenty-First was that they had Gunner Bricker, a world class hacker who had been trained by the wife of the greatest hacker to ever invade the internet.

Within twenty-four hours of receiving the DNA results, every repository of DNA information was being hacked and cross referenced from the computers in Texas. The results surprised those observing the search as the first result came from the DNA Identification Pool of the French Foreign Legion.

The individual the DNA belonged to was shown as Miguel Sanchez, and he was listed as Killed in Action three years earlier during a United Nations operation in the Congo. Since members of the Legion did not serve under their real names, Gunner Bricker hacked into the personnel records of the Legion to discover his real name was Luis Manuel Ortega from El Salvador.

Lieutenant Colonel Garcia smiled when they received the El Salvadoran records on Ortega as they showed him to be wanted in coordination with a crack-down on drug and human trafficking which the Twenty-First had played a part in several years prior to this incident. The information was kicked back to the Mossad whom then contacted the Foreign Legion and advised them to make the announcement themselves since it would come out within a few days and this way they would not look as if they are trying to hide anything from the world.

Once the information was released, the Mossad released a statement that they would provide any assistance requested in the investigation into the attack on Mecca, but would not take an active part since several countries were still trying to place the blame on the Israeli's. What they did not tell the world was that they were sending a deep cover agent to the Twenty-First to team up with one of their people in an attempt to locate and remove the people behind the attack.

Recall

For Josh and Delores, they finally figured out how to get out of the condo and do things as a couple with her dressing down and adding a wig to change her hair style and color. Josh watched the news when she was out taking care of her business but had turned his phone off since he was on leave, using her house phone to contact his unit every couple of days to see if they were going to activate with him being recalled from leave.

In Texas they had a different problem. Who were they going to team the Mossad agent up with? They needed an independent operator who spoke both Spanish and Farsi. Josh's name kept coming up.

When General Grainger ordered Josh to be activated and to report to the Twenty-First, it was quickly noticed that his phone was off. His unit was contacted and discovered he was on leave, with the only location noted on his leave papers was Los Angeles. Intelligence first tried to ping his phone's GPS Locator without success, so they then went after his vehicles GPS with success. Both Sandra and Gloria smiled at the location given for Josh's vehicle. It was parked in from of Delores Ramirez's condo.

Gloria had an idea on how to get Josh's attention which made Sandra chuckle. One dozen Tiger Lilies were ordered for delivery to Delores Ramirez at her home without a card by a local florist.

The first five days that Josh spent with Delores was one long frantic sexual encounter when she was home. But the sixth day, sex just happened when she desired it and Delores had begun to wear one of his t-shirts around the house instead of just her panties.

It was the fifteenth day of their co-habitation when Delores was studying a script for a television sitcom when her doorbell rang. When she answered the door, a florist deliveryman just handed her a crystal vase with a dozen Tiger Lilies, nodded and left her standing in the door wondering what they were all about since she had never had flowers delivered to her home before.

When she closed the door and turned around, she saw Josh standing across the room, looking at her.

"Josh, do you know anything about this? Did you order these?"

"They're not for you Delores, they are a message meant for me."

"A message for you? I don't understand?"

He stood for a moment thinking before answering her.

"Delores, the people who sent me to Samoa, wants me to contact them, meaning I have a new mission."

"But you're on leave."

He walked to her and placed his hands on her shoulders.

"Delores, listen carefully. The people who sent those flowers are not the regular military. They are part of the Special Operations Command, and when they call, I have two choices. Go or tell them no. But they would not call unless it is very important. I cannot say anymore without violating security, and even possibly endangering you at the same time."

He took the vase from her hands and walked over to the coffee table and sat them down. She was standing next to him when he turned back to her.

"How soon do you have to leave?" She asked.

"Let me make a phone call then I'll know more."

"Do we have time for us?"

Josh smiled.

"Go get the bed warmed up while I make the call."

Josh left at four the next morning with his groin aching and very little sleep from the night before. Neither had said any words of love only that they would miss each other. He told her not to wait for him, for her to find someone stable to grow old with. She told him to let her know when he was in the area and unless she had found that one person, they could still enjoy a night or three together.

He drove to Casa Grande, Arizona and spent the rest of the day and night with his parents before going on to Texas. Josh left them with half the money he had taken from Samoa, telling them he had been playing high stakes poker and that is where the money had came from, just to not try to deposit it since the bank would have to report such a large sum of money and they'd not only have to pay taxes on it, he would be in trouble with the Marines for getting into those games.

Josh arrived at the compound of the Twenty-First just after nine in the evening as he had driven all day, leaving before daylight. He was directed to go directly to the Bunker and report in. He was taken directly to the conference room where people were working, and he looked at the large wall monitor to see what was happening in the world.

The number of deaths being reported world-wide shocked him as the media was not reporting this information. Josh had been watching the data stream on the monitor for about five minutes when a voice spoke to him from his left.

"Glad to see you could make it Captain Kramer."

He turned to see Gloria Garcia standing there in civilian clothes.

"Colonel Garcia, what's with the Captain comment?"

"When you get your briefing packet, you'll find your orders from Headquarters, Marine Corps promoting you to Captain in it. Congratulations on your promotion."

"Thank you, Ma'am. Now what am I doing here if you do not mind?"

"The Israeli's are taking a beating on this situation at Mecca and they've asked for our help. We need someone with language skills, in Spanish and Farsi, and your name popped. I hope we have not messed up anything with Miss Ramirez?"

"Two ships passing in the night as the saying goes. It was fun but could not last as we live in very different worlds. So, where is the package so I can get started on it?"

She moved to the conference room table and picked up a folder that had to be over an inch thick and handed it too him. He opened it up and looked at the first page then spoke to Garcia.

"Colonel, I picked up an extra package in Samoa, that was not in my report."

"I know about the money, forget it. Gunny DeMello told me about it. Call it a bonus for a job well done."

"Thank you but I need something done with it or what's left of it, that I think the Group could help with."

"What's that?"

"I have a hundred thousand that I want to make sure gets into the hands of my old Gunny. Gunnery Sergeant Conway."

"He's in Long Beach, isn't he?"

"Yes Ma'am, he is."

"I'll put a bug in the Sergeant Major's ear. You give him the money and he'll make sure Gunny Conway gets the funds without the government asking any questions."

"Thanks. Now am I in a team house or bungalow?"

"Bungalow Nine."

"Well if you'll excuse me, I need to get my gear unloaded and grab some sleep as I've been on the go since 0400."

It was after eleven before he was able to put his head down for the night. For a brief moment he thought of Delores, then put her out of his mind. It would serve no purpose to think about her as he had told the Colonel, they were just passing through and enjoyed each other for that brief period.

Josh was up at five and ran four miles before going over to the weight room and spending two hours working out before heading to the Hospital's Cafeteria for breakfast.

He sat and watched the late morning crowd come and go in the cafeteria wondering if he might find time to go to the canteen and maybe get lucky with one of the females of the unit. It wasn't that he felt the need to get laid, it was a vague hope he could forget about Delores.

Josh spent the afternoon reading the briefing packet and laying it out by date or subject matter. Four of the six men had been identified, all with criminal pasts. One had even been reported killed by Drug Enforcement Agents three years before the attack on Mecca. The most obvious thing was an operation of this nature would require a lot of money, then the facilities to mutate the virus into a stronger, resistant bug. That would require very expensive equipment and highly skill personnel to do the work.

The last thing was a location to do the work without fear of discovery. Work? That had to include the cosmetic surgery on the attackers. Then there was the logistics of moving everything to Saudi Arabia. The truck was the easy part since it was registered to a German Aid Organization working in Yemen and had been reported missing or stolen nearly five weeks before the attack.

From what he could gather from the packet, he was to team up with an Israeli agent, find the source of the attack and remove the threat of it happening again. The packet never told him exactly who he would be teamed with.

Josh took the briefing packet and the money to the Sergeant Major before the end of the day to insure neither was lying around his bungalow. He ate in the Bunker's Cafeteria before going back to his place to think. The only thing that made sense was he was going to be sent out to eliminate a target since he was not part of the intelligence network within the Twenty-First or the Marine Corps. He knew how to gather intelligence, but interpretation was not in his resume.

He got cleaned up and decided that a beer and maybe pleasant conversation at the Canteen would be a nice idea. Josh was not thinking on getting lucky with one of the Group's females even though he had experience with a couple of them from previous trips to the Compound, he just wanted out of the bungalow.

There were several rules that were common knowledge about the Canteen. No talk about operations, past or pending. Limitations on consumption of alcohol was strictly enforced. And the females of the Group selected their bed partners if they so desired one. At no time could a man even hint to the possibility of taking one of the ladies to bed, and he could even say no to the prospect once it was mentioned by a female, although this was a rare occurrence.

The Canteen was not as busy as it normally was since the Bunker personnel was working long shifts gathering and processing information on the attack on Mecca. Josh grabbed a beer at the bar then went to a vacant table to just watch the activity. Soon he was joined by a female named Betty who was a Lab Tech at the hospital then a few minutes later, Mary, one of the cooks from the Bunker's Cafeteria joined them.

As was typical with all of the females in the Group, they were in good shape and had nice bodies. These were also two that Josh was not familiar with from previous trips to the Group Compound. He danced with both females but neither had yet to make an advance towards a bedroom.

Josh had been at the Canteen over an hour when it seemed the gravitational pull of the place centered on the door and what had walked through it.

Standing just inside the door was a female wearing a black tube dress that barely covering her lower assets and she was wearing heels causing the muscles in her legs to stand out to give them a perfect shape. The top of the dress barely covered her breasts and it was obvious she was not wearing a bra.

She had long, black hair framing her heart shaped face. Her complexion was dark, but not black as her facial features were that of a Caucasian. Even across the room her blue eyes stood out from her face and her modestly full lips were covered in rose colored lip gloss.

There was no doubt in anyone's mind that this female had just pushed the dress code for the Canteen to the maximum limit.

Josh heard Mary mutter that this new female looked good enough to eat. He looked at Mary who shrugged her shoulders then spoke again.

"Josh, I'm straight, but if that offered, I think I'd have to try it out just to see if what is being advertised is worth the effort."

Josh chuckled and when he looked back at the door, he found that the new female was moving directly towards his table. She stopped a step from the table, looked at both females occupying the table with Josh before speaking. But when she spoke, she spoke Farsi without a touch of accent.

"Captain Kramer I presume?"

"Yes, and you are?" He replied in Farsi.

She cocked her head then smiled.

"The music is nice, take me around the dance floor once or twice." This time she spoke Spanish, again without an accent.

Josh nodded, excused himself from the ladies at the table then moved around to take this new females hand. Once in the middle of the dance floor, she spoke to him in English with what Josh considered a slight Russian accent.

"My name is Tatiana Chipovskaya. Captain Tatiana Chipovskaya of the Mossad. My friends call me Tina. We are to partner together according to General Grainger."

"And you dress like this to meet me? Care to explain your thinking here?"

"Certainly. From what I have been told about the procedures for finding a lover here at the Canteen, we are going to leave together once this song is over and start working on getting to know each other. And no, not in bed. But I have moved into your spare bedroom while you were here enjoying the other ladies."

"And what if I have plans with one of them tonight in my own bed?"

"From the looks everyone in this place are giving us, do you think the night will turn out any other way?"

She moved closer to his body, pressing her chest against his. He responded by shifting his arms around her without placing them in a compromising position.

"Well, it seems your logic has won the day. Are you wearing anything at all under that dress?"

"Nothing at all."

"Damn!"

When the dance ended, she once again took his hand and they walked out of the Canteen without further comment to anyone present. As they were walking to his bungalow, she broke the silence.

"Josh. I may call you Josh, can't I?"

"Certainly Tina."

"Good. Anyway, we need to change because as soon as we can, we need to get to your Fun House and begin training, getting to know each other in a tactical way."

"Then why the costume?"

"The dress? I was just wanting to have a bit of fun and I don't always get to dress in such a fashion."

In the bungalow, she went directly to the spare bedroom and closed the door, Josh looked at the door for several moments before he went to his room and got dressed. He exited his room to find her standing against her door frame with her hair pulled back and tied into a ponytail and her lips were clean of any lip gloss.

She was armed as he was and ready to go. He motioned towards the door and she led the way. Once outside she took off at a jog and he quickly caught up with her as they jogged to the Fun House.

They were met at the Fun House by the Sergeant Major who just looked at his watch then pointed to the first door. Josh took the door with Tina following. Room after room was taken with them leap frogging until they ended up back in the perimeter corridor at the end of the eighth room with the Sergeant Major waiting on them with a PAD in his hands as he looked at the results of the run.

"Captain Chipovskaya, not bad for your first run through our little Fun House." The Sergeant Major commented.

"Well, it seemed like you had it set up for a beginner." She replied.

"Captain, that was the Bravo Five Course." Was the Sergeant Major's response to her comment.

"Sergeant Major load up Charlie Nine." Josh instructed.

The Sergeant Major looked at Josh, then Tina.

"Alright. It'll take about thirty minutes, go reload and take a break. I'll let you know when it's ready."

Josh guided Tina back to a room where they could reload their magazines and take a break. She discovered there was a commercial coffee service there with hot water and a selection of tea bags. Tina quickly made a cup of tea using one of the cups that were upside down on a white towel, then began to reload her magazines from one of the dozen, open ammunition cans on a table across the room.

As she was reloading, Josh came to her and laid out a set of foam ear plugs and a new silencer for her pistol.

"Let me have your weapon." He instructed.

She pulled her weapon, cleared and checked it before handing it over to him. Josh took a spanner wrench from a pocket on his vest and loosened the silencer with it before spinning it off. He put the new one on, tighten it, then handed the weapon back to her.

"Make sure you put the ear plugs in cause it can get real loud running this next course." He advised her.

She looked at him wondering what he meant by loud while using silencers but did as she was told.

Tina put the earplugs in, then finished reloading her magazines. She just leaned back against the table as she sipped on her tea, waiting for the call to return to the rooms. She didn't have long to wait.

Josh took the first door and Tina quickly learned this was going to be a much harder course of fire. She took the second door with Josh moving past her as he was firing. Tina started to turn towards the next door when a movement caught her eye and as she turned back to her left to take a new target that had turned around to face her, she felt something hit her in her left breast, causing a painful sting then a loud gunshot.

As she was looking down at her breast, Josh swung on her target and eliminated it then moved to her side.

53

"Listen to me. That's a paintball. Every room has paintball guns on laser tracking gimbals. From the time the target turns you have three seconds to hit it or the paintball gun fires based upon the laser tracking. Now let's move it, we can worry about getting hit later."

They took five more rooms and it was not hard for Josh to notice her getting hit shook her up as her performance declined. They exited out into the perimeter corridor to find not only the Sergeant Major, but Lieutenant Colonel Garcia waiting for them.

Garcia stepped to Tina and ran her finger through the paint on her breast, then on her left shoulder. Tina had been hit three times with another hit to her back at her right shoulder. Josh had been hit once in his back from a shot that missed Tina, but got him instead.

"Captain Kramer, care to explain why you had the Charlie Nine course set up?"

"Colonel Garcia let me say that I felt Captain Chipovskaya was a bit smug after running a Bravo Course. And since my briefing packet states I am the senior officer on this detail, we'll run the Charlie Nine Course until we complete it with neither of us having paint on our uniform."

Garcia looked at him for several seconds then asked a question he knew was coming if not in form, but intent.

"Do you tell her about the Charlie Nine or do I?"

"Be my guest Colonel."

"Captain Chipovskaya, the Charlie Nine course is designed for a team of four or more shooters, not two. There are not but a handful of operators that can run the course with only a single partner. Captain Kramer is one of those as is the Sergeant Major."

Tina looked hard at Garcia, trying to hide the feelings she had coursing through her body, and the realization that if this had been real, she would be dead.

"Colonel, have you ran it this way?"

"Yes, I have. And the first three times I ran it, I was covered in paint. Get with the program Captain, it's for your own good."

Garcia started to turn away when Josh spoke up.

"Colonel, whose idea was it for the two of us to bunk together?"

Garcia looked at Josh without smiling.

"Mine. To be honest, we did not know who the Mossad was sending until she got off the plane. The airfield support personnel already had instructions to put her in your bungalow so as she reported in, her baggage was moved to your bungalow. The two of you will have to play the part of a couple so I decided to leave her there as it will be a good way to get to know one another and become comfortable around each other. It was not so the two of you could share a single bed, although once in the field, you may have to in playing your parts. You're both professionals and I expect both of you to work hard in developing a common ground with each other. Am I clear on this?"

"Crystal Colonel, thank you."

"Captain Chipovskaya?"

"Yes Ma'am."

"Good, now go reload, then go get some rest."

Tina never spoke to Josh as they went back to reload their magazines as per policy that all magazines would be full at all times even in quarters. Josh watched as her hands shook as she pressed each round into the magazines until she was ready to go back to the bungalow.

At the bungalow he opened the door for her and she went in directly to her room and closed the door. Josh just shrugged his shoulders and went to his to shower then bed as it was now after midnight. He was standing next to his bed, nude, about to put on a fresh pair of boxer shorts when his door opened, and Tina was standing there in a bra and panties with her hair wet from showering.

"Did you intend to humiliate me in front of the Colonel?"

As he stepped into his boxers, he answered her.

"No Tina, I did not, but I was asked a question and I answered it honestly. It's a fault I have about giving direct responses to direct questions."

"But you did have us run that last course to put me in my place." It was not a question but a statement.

"Yes, I suppose I did. Listen, your actions, your comments after that first run was almost as if your were an adult speaking down to a child. I don't know your background, but mine is in the leadership of men in combat. Twice in Afghanistan and once in Pakistan, plus seven missions for the Twenty-First. I've lost men in combat, good men that maybe if I had pushed them harder they'd still be alive. But one thing is certain Captain Chipovskaya, I'm not going to loose you because you do not measure up to my standards. So, get with the program as the Colonel said, or go home. Am I clear on this?"

"And if I don't measure up? What, you go it alone?"

"Captain, the nice thing about the Twenty-First is, until we leave this compound, I can cancel my part in the operation. Go back to Camp Pendleton and take over a company of Marines. The Operational Plan calls for two people, not one and I'll not go this one alone, but I do need someone I can trust and know will have my back when the shit hits the fan."

She stood looking at him for over a minute without commenting, then turned away for her room. Josh thought another time and place, she would be a fireball in bed. He walked to his door, turned out the bedroom light and left his door open as he went to bed.

Josh was sitting at the kitchen table at six the next morning sipping on a cup of coffee when Tina exited her room dressed in Neon Blue stain running shorts with matching tank top, showing a red halter beneath that. She looked at Josh then walked to the front door. Josh sat his cup down and followed her, catching up with her on the front porch as she was looking around, trying to determine which way to go for her run.

He never said a word to her as he stepped past her, went off the porch and began jogging away from the people who were out for their morning runs. Seconds later, she came up beside him and matched his easy pace. The morning pre-dawn light was enough for them to see the road they were running on as they left the main part of the compound with Josh taking them out towards the ranges.

They past the ranges and continued their run until he brought them to the Basic Obstacles Course. Josh did not attempt to take the course at the beginning, but by-passed those obstacles and went to the rock climbing wall in the middle and without speaking to Tina, started up the wall.

He was about a third of the way up the wall when he looked back to see her standing at the bottom.

"Move it Captain, we don't have all day." He advised her.

The look she gave him would have melted an iceberg, but Josh just ignored it as he scrambled to the top of the forty foot wall then sat, straddling the top waiting for her. When she topped the wall, she looked over it to see a cargo net hanging down the other side. Josh just smiled at her, then dropped over the edge, catching the net and worked his way down it as quickly as possible.

Tina took a deep breath and carefully went over the side of the wall and worked her way down the net, missing her footing twice but held on to regain it then went to the next rung on the net until she finally made the bottom. She stood looking at him, then at the rest of the course, wondering what he had planned for her to do next.

What happened next surprised her in that he never spoke to her, but turned and walked back to the road with her following a few steps behind him. He never attempted to jog or even pick up the pace he was walking at as she caught up to him. She finally spoke to him as they came upon the first pistol range.

"Captain Kramer, what's this all about? This run and obstacle course now walking back to our quarters?"

He stopped then turned to her causing her to also stop.

"Captain Chipovskaya, Tina, let's go back to last nights conversation. I need to know the condition you are in, so I can plan our training to get us out of here as quickly as possible. It's three miles plus a bit from our quarters to the obstacle course and we did that at a leisurely pace telling me you could have made it in half the time if necessary. Second that wall scares a lot of new people as does the net on the other side because there is no safety lines or nets to catch you if you fall."

He paused for a moment.

"Now you could have told me to go screw myself at the wall and to be honest, I would not have thought less of you since you are not on the payroll of the Twenty-First, or even in our military. I want you to consider that from now on. We have to get you up to speed with a handgun, so I do not have to worry about my back if things go to hell on us. That's the only real training we need to accomplish from this moment on. If you wish to run in the morning, go for it, otherwise we focus on firearms training. Do you have a problem with my training concept?"

"Yes, I'm hungry, now shut up and let's go get cleaned up then get something to eat."

She never gave him a chance to respond when she took off at a run, faster than they had came out this way. Josh laughed then caught up to her and let her set the pace. They were within sight of the bungalow when Tina asked a question of Josh.

"Josh, I understand all operators have nicknames for call signs. What's yours?"

"They call me the Wizard."

Tina came to an immediate stop with Josh taking several more steps before stopping and turning back to her."

"What's wrong?"

"Are you the one that did the job in Santiago Chile last year?"

He walked back to her and just looked hard into her eyes before answering.

"I don't know how you know about Santiago, but yes, that was me, and that is also the last time you ask me about any operation I may or may not have been part of. Do I make myself clear?"

"Yes, very clear. I'm sorry."

"Tina, it seems no one told you that such things are not discussed outside of the senior staff and the operators, and even then, it is very rare when that might happen. You are not part of this command, you are an adjunct, so do yourself a favor and forget anything you may have heard about this Group and this place."

As he turned to walk away, she grabbed his arm, stopping him.

"One final thing Captain Josh Kramer. I was given the option of walking from this project if I felt my team mate was not up to the standards I have become used too. We both know there are people who excel in training, yet their combat performance never seems to come up to that same level. I was honestly considering scrubbing this mission and going home until you told me your nickname. How I know about Santiago is a question that shall remain unanswered, but knowing it was you, has changed my thinking on all of this. I'm staying with the mission. Now you can stop playing games, and I'll bust my ass to get up to your standards. If you scrub this mission, it won't be because I haven't tried."

He could see something in her eyes that told him she was almost pleading with him to stay the course.

"Alright then. Now we go get cleaned up, something to eat, then we work out as tight a training schedule as possible. The longer it takes to get into the field, the more time the other side has to cover their tracks. Let's go."

They did not speak again until inside the bungalow when she went to her bedroom door.

"Josh…" She pushed her bedroom door open. "The Colonel expects us to act like a couple on this mission. No closed doors from here on unless you wish company for the night from one of the ladies at the Canteen. This is not an invite, but we both need to get used to one another in various levels of dress or undress."

Josh nodded his head.

"Alright, I see your point, and if you wish company, let me know, and I'll give you all the privacy possible."

Tina started to speak, then just turned and walked into her room. Josh caught that slight pause and wondered what that was about, then shook it out of his head and went to shower.

Exposure

Josh was lacing his boots up when he heard metal on metal noise as if someone was in the kitchen setting pans on the stove. He finished what he was doing and left his uniform blouse lying on the bed when he went to investigate the noise. Two steps out of his room and he came to a sudden stop as he saw Tina at the stove.

Her hair was wrapped up under a towel, but what she was wearing was not meant for daily wear or even underwear unless the intent was to end the night on the bedroom floor.

Tina was wearing what it took Josh several seconds to remember was called a Teddy. Except this one was white and nearly transparent. At the bottom it was French Cut, barely covering her ass and the back was open nearly to the crack of her ass. He figured if he was looking at her front, nothing would be hidden, alerting whomever viewed her what they could expect once if came off her body.

Josh turned back into his room and went to his dresser and removed an old football jersey, then took it too Tina. She turned to him as he moved to her and there was no doubt about certain aspects of her body. He did not look down to see where heaven resided, only at her face.

"Here, put this on." He instructed.

"Is there something wrong with what I'm wearing?"

"Other than the fact you may as well be nude, several things. Please put this on."

She looked at the jersey and spoke as she slipped in on. With her arms over her head her breasts became even more accented and Josh looked away.

"There, that better?"

"Yes. Look I understand about what you said as far as seeing each other in various forms of undress, but this is not acceptable. What if someone knocked on the door? You'd have to go into your room and hide, or put something on as I answered the door, plus you have food cooking on the stove, which would probably burn while all of that was going on."

"Yes, you are right. I just grabbed the first thing I saw in my dresser. Is that all?"

"Don't let the ham burn."

He turned away from her knowing he was about to put his foot in his mouth about the way she looked. Her dark Middle Eastern complexion framed in white was causing him to rethink how he related to her, especially since Delores often dressed that way.

She served up scrambled eggs with hash browns and ham steaks. As they began eating he posed a question to her.

"I thought Jews had a prohibition against eating ham or any type of pork?"

"As a race, we do, but one thing to watch for is people who avoid eating pork, especially with my complexion. That means they are either a Jew or Muslim, and when working undercover, it's not a good idea to expose yourself to much. Besides, I like ham."

"I guess that makes sense. So, when in public, I need to remember to treat you as if you are an American, Russian, Mexican, or what?"

"Josh, I can clean my accent up to just about any dialect you think we need or as our cover says we need, but with your

Southwestern accent, American or Mexican probably works best. Let's wait and see what the Colonel has for us."

They discussed training, mostly with firearms and explosives as they ate with Tina giving him the information on her own Mossad training. As they were finishing up breakfast, the house phone rang, with Josh getting up to answer it.

"Kramer."

(Pause)

"Okay Sergeant Major, we'll be right there."

(Pause)

"Oh. Alright. I'll be there as soon as I finish dressing."

He turned to Tina as he hung up the phone.

"Colonel Garcia wants to see me, so I'd best get going. Put the dishes in the sink and I'll wash them when I get back if possible, or later. You cooked, I wash."

"Okay Josh sounds like a deal."

Colonel Garcia had him close the door when he entered her office than handed him a red folder with a document stapled to the cover and an ink pen clipped to it. She told him to sit and read then sign the cover document. The document told him he had Tina's official Mossad records in his hands. He signed the document, clipped the pen to it, then opened the folder up. From page one he began to get upset with what he was reading.

The file was nearly a half inch thick and he read every page. Based upon what the file said on Tina, he was glad that the only photos of her in it were stock photos for identification. When he finished the file, he just closed it up and looked at Garcia for a moment before speaking.

"When did this file come in?"

"It came in while you and the Captain were playing on the obstacle course. It came in via electronic transmission and I had to use an agreed upon password I have with the Mossad concerning such electronic exchanges. No one has seen that file except for me and Gunner Bricker."

"So, you knew where we were at the time it came in. Are you having her watched?"

"Of course, she is or was an unknown. If you were in any danger at any time during your morning exercises, she would have been dealt with."

Josh laughed.

"Sure, but she sleeps in the same bungalow with me, so who is protecting me inside our quarters?"

"An accident on the obstacle course is one thing, killing you in your sleep is another. She's a professional, she'd know better than to try that trick."

"Yeah, I'm too young and in too good of shape to claim I had a heart attack during sex."

Garcia tilted her head in a questioning manner. Josh chuckled.

"No Colonel, that has not already happened and even before I came in here, I had no plans for such a thing although she and I have brushed over the subject of sleeping together, sleeping in the same bed once we leave here as part of our cover."

"Well, blood was drawn last night before she came to get your from the Canteen. She's clean and as her file shows, she has a current implant. That risk is off the table."

Josh just nodded his head as she continued.

"First of all, the information in that file cannot leave this office, which means you do not talk to her about any of it. Second, how do you wish to deal with this?"

"Colonel, I'm just a dumb Captain. Your call here but let's see how things work out in training."

She looked at him for a second before responding.

"If you were a dumb Captain, you'd not be sitting there. But I want you to send her over to see me when you return to the bungalow. She needs to know we have her records, so she does not try something stupid."

"Not sure about stupid, but this morning on the way back from the obstacle course, I found out from her that she knew it was me in Santiago, but she never told me how she knew that. All she said was she knew it was the Wizard that did that job. Colonel, from her file, she was never near South America when that went down, so how did she find out about it and my call sign?"

"I think I need that information PDQ then get Gunner Bricker on it even quicker. Someone is ease dropping in on our communications which means our coding is scrammed. Send her to me."

"Alright Colonel. Anything else?"

"No. You're dismissed."

When Josh walked into the bungalow, he found Tina dressed for whatever activity that was planned for the rest of the day.

"Josh, I went ahead and washed the dishes since there were so few. What did the Colonel want?"

"She wants you in her office, otherwise we talked training."

"I wonder why she wants to see me again so soon?"

"You'll have to ask her."

When Tina tapped on the Colonel's door frame, she was told to come in and take a seat, but she was not told to close the door. Garcia rose up enough from her chair and handed Tina's Mossad file over to her. There was no hiding the look on Tina's face when she read the cover page including Josh's signature on the form.

Garcia never spoke as Tina opened the file. Tina knew from the first page what the file most likely held and looked at Garcia.

"So, Captain Kramer has read my file?"

"Yes, he has, and he has been ordered not to speak of it to anyone, including you. Now first, turn around and look behind you."

Tina turned to see the Sergeant Major and a Marine wearing a nametag telling all his name was DeMello.

"Captain, you will read your file and you will advise me of every little thing that has been removed from it or doctored. Once that is complete, you will also advise me how you knew it was the Wizard who did the job in Santiago. If you do not cooperate, there is a medic outside with a syringe of a nice little concoction developed by your own Mossad that will make you tell the truth no matter how hard you try not to. Do we have an understanding here?"

"Colonel, there is no need for the medic. If you will check the files on Santiago, you will note that one Diego Sanchez traveled to Moscow every couple of months on business. He also liked young, fit females and since I look much younger than I really am, it was just a matter of putting me in the right place for him to discover me, then making sure he wanted more of the same when he returned again."

She paused for a second.

"If he was in Moscow for a week, I'd be with him day and night, often meeting him at the airport when he arrived. Our conversations would be in broken English for my part and he never knew I spoke Spanish. This gave me the ability to basically listen in on several of his conversations as his Moscow contacts did speak Spanish and they would converse that way as a means of hiding what they were doing."

Garcia turned to her computer and began typing in commands.

"Go ahead Captain, I'm listening."

"We were not after him as much as his Moscow contacts since he was not involved in supplying weapons to Palestine. But those he was working with were involved and we needed more information on who was involved before we took any action."

Tina could see folders showing on Garcia's monitor then photos. Even from the angle Tina was looking, she could see photos of herself appearing with Sanchez's.

"Oh God Colonel, you're not going to show Captain Kramer those photos, are you?"

"Do I need too?"

"Not if he has read this file."

"Alright, go on with your report on Moscow."

"My contact was another Mossad agent posing as a client. Sanchez wasn't the only individual in the group we were watching, and it was through him that I was able to get close to several others. Several days after Captain Kramer accomplished his mission in Santiago, my contact met me for an afternoon appointment as we always did, and he told me that Sanchez was dead and only that an operator that went by the callsign Wizard had done the deed. From there I later looked up the incident on the internet and read the specifics there. I really do not know how my contact received the information he passed on to me."

Garcia scanned several photos before closing the folder.

"Okay, now your file."

Tina went through the file page by page only commenting on minor details which Garcia was not concerned about. It took over an hour before Tina closed her file and told Garcia that was everything.

"Thank you, Captain. Now those two men behind you are deaf and dumb meaning whatever they heard here today will never reach their lips, and believe me when I say they hold greater secrets than yours. I'm going to call Tel Aviv in a few minutes and have a nice long talk with your folks which you have no need to hear."

"Yes Ma'am."

"You're dismissed."

Tina stood and handed her file back to Garcia then turned for the door stopping to speak once more.

"Colonel, I don't know why Tel Aviv sent me here, but I'd like to stay and learn more from Captain Kramer."

"That's as much up to him as your people in Tel Aviv."

"Thank you, Colonel."

When Tina walked into the bungalow, Josh was at the table with a note pad writing down whatever he was working on. She only paused a second before going into her room. From the angle that Josh was sitting, he could look into her room and saw she had placed one of her bags on the bed and had opened it. He watched for a minute as she began to pull her things from her dresser and was placing them in the bag. He got up and went to her door.

"What are you doing Tina?"

"Leaving."

"May I ask why?"

She stood and looked at him in disbelief.

"Are you kidding me? You read my file. Do you want to put your life in my hands?"

"I saw a dedicated agent who preformed their assignments in a highly professional manner despite adverse conditions."

"My God Josh, I spent more time on my back than I did upright. I've never had to use a firearm in any manner even if I am fairly capable of handling one. I'm untested."

"Then why did you accept the assignment?"

"Using a Hollywood term, I was being type casted as a whore, to be used to seduce men and a few women into telling me their deep, dark secrets while in bed. Do you realize that most men and women who use a prostitute really want to have human contact as much as sexual contact? Once they feel comfortable with their playmate, they are liable to say anything, often just to get the guilt off their chest. You killed one of my clients in Santiago, a man who did not know I could speak Spanish and he often confessed, used me as a priest, speaking in Spanish about what he was doing. I played the dumb Russian bimbo and just smiled as he spoke to me."

She paused and took a deep breath before continuing.

"I accepted this assignment to prove to myself and my superiors that I am a good agent and can perform outside a bedroom. And I don't mean giving blow jobs in the back of a limo."

"Alright, I can buy that, but why the hooker approach last night and that nearly nothing Teddy this morning?"

"When I was shown your photo last night I developed an itch. You're an attractive man Josh Kramer and even prostitutes need to feel the touch of a man who is not paying for the privilege. I figured once we had gone through the shooting program the Colonel ordered for us, I could enjoy a man for the night without the trauma or suspicion that goes with what I had been doing. I have not been with a man for nearly six months and a girl gets used to such activity after a while, even if she is being paid to perform. After finding out you are the Wizard, I wanted that even more just to feel like a woman again, and not just a piece of meat."

Josh barely hesitated before he spoke again, this time like a commanding officer.

"Captain Chipovskaya, you will unpack that bag and join me in writing our training schedule, so we can get this show on the road. We don't have time for this right now. If intelligence gets a break on this situation and we have to deploy, I need to know you are ready, both physically and mentally. We are burning daylight there."

He started to turn away from her then turned back.

"For your information, I don't put out on the first date, so take a cold shower or buy batteries, the choice is yours."

Tina could not help but laugh at his battery comment as she just looked at her bag then followed him to the table.

Colonel Garcia looked up from her desk at the Sergeant Major standing in the doorway.

"What Michael?"

"It's been over an hour and neither of them have returned and no call for a medic. I think you are right in that Josh is going to go with what he was given to work with. I only hope he can glue her back together cause she is certainly broken."

"We all are Michael. That's what makes this unit so special."

He stood for a moment pondering his next statement.

"Gloria, you need to retire the Black Orchid. Find a good man and start enjoying life once again. Little Marco will soon be ten and before you know it, he'll be gone, than your last anchor will be gone, leaving you to rust away."

"Since when have you become a philosopher?"

"Since Donna chipped away the rust that was building up on me. I'm serious Gloria, you are one of the best operators I've ever seen, but you keep pushing your luck, you're gonna leave Marco without a mother."

"Thank you, Michael, is there anything else?"

"No, only as soon as Captain Kramer gives me a schedule, I'll set up his range times."

Unusual Comforts

It had been a rough two days after Tina had read her own file as Josh had them on ranges nearly around the clock, bringing her up to his standards. They had just completed the fourth run in the Fun House and she was aching in several places where paintballs had impacted her unarmored body. Josh said he did not want her use to wearing body armor since it was every likely they would not be in a position to get armored up before a fight.

She was standing in her room, nude as she dried off from her shower when Josh stepped into her doorway. He could see the bruises on her body, especially her breasts from the paintballs.

"Tina are you alright?"

"Other than feeling like a punching bag, no. What am I doing wrong?"

"You're trying too hard for one. Turn your mind off and just let it flow. You have the principles down and actually your shooting is near Colonel Garcia's ability, but you are tense. Relax, it'll come to you."

"I'll try. Still no word from Intelligence?"

"You'll know as soon as I know. Now get some rest. A short run in the morning then I want you in the whirlpool to help ease those aches you are feeling from getting hit with the paintballs."

He turned away from her before she could respond. She dried off, then put on regular panties and a sports bra so she would not be rolling about in bed on her bruised breasts. She stood for a moment then pulled out a set of pajamas and put them on before turning her light out and walking to Josh's bedroom.

She caught him coming out of his bathroom only wearing boxers when she entered his room, walked to his bed and pulled the covers back before crawling into it. He looked at her for a moment before she spoke to him.

"This is not an invite and I'm not coming out of these clothes, but it would be nice to have something to snuggle up against besides a pillow tonight."

He stepped to his dresser, opened a drawer and pulled out a t-shirt and put it on, then rummaged around until he found a pair of sleep pants and put them on.

"Fair's fair isn't it?"

She laughed and laid her head down on the pillow as she watched him get into bed. Once he was settled in, she curled up next to him as he was facing away from her, laid an arm over him and let sleep take her.

The next morning found them in opposite positions with him up against her and when the alarm went off and woke her, she felt a hardness against her that she knew she wanted, but was not going to force the issue. His arm was over her, and as he started to remove it, she grabbed it and held him in place, moving his hand to her breast.

They just lay like that for several minutes as the alarm clock was making racket, telling them it was time to get up. She rolled around under his arm until she was facing him. Then gave him a quick peck on his lips.

"Thank you, we can get up now."

"Is that what you want?" He asked her.

"No, I want that racket off and other noise to fill this room."

"Tina, I'll make you a deal. You complete the Charlie Nine without getting yourself or me splattered with paint and we can do this without all of the insulation both of us are wearing."

"Is that a bribe?"

"Call it what you want."

"You have a deal. Now turn that damn racket off, get up, cause that firmness I feel between your legs is bothering me."

Josh laughed, and rolled away from her, turned off the alarm as he stood up, then offered his hand to help her out of bed. When her feet hit the floor, he pulled her to him and looked at her a moment before he leaned over and kissed her hard. She wrapped her arms around him as his right hand went to her ass and grabbed it hard, pulling her up and tighter to his body.

When they broke the kiss, he released her and stepped back smiling.

"You bastard." She took a playful swipe at him with her hand as she laughed then turned and walked out of his bedroom for her own.

That night she was only hit once during two runs through the Fun House and he never received a single hit. She came to his bed once again dressed in pajamas but when he came to bed, he was nude. She never said a thing as she snuggled up to him.

When they awoke she had her hand on him as she edged up and kissed him as he had kissed her the previous morning. She broke the kiss, then moved down to his erection and took him with her mouth. Neither spoke as he laid there enjoying her talent until he was spent. When she finished him, she just got up and walked out of the bedroom without speaking to him.

Neither commented on her actions that day and even though she took another hit in the Fun House, she came to bed naked, with her going to sleep with her head on his shoulder without any further sexual contact except for the flesh against flesh.

The next two days were spent working with explosives and running the Master Obstacle Course where obstacles had to be blown up to navigate the course. Tina proved to be very proficient with explosives and showed a high level of training in judging what had to be done with them.

She was still sleeping nude with Josh but except for that one morning, she never made another overt move on him as they slept together. He had set conditions for their coupling and because of other requirements and teams needing the Fun House, they had not ran the course during the time afterwards.

They had been together for nearly two weeks as she progressed each trip to the Fun House getting better with each run at the course. Other than the one morning where she took him orally, there was no other sexual contact other than sleeping together nude.

They had just completed a four mile run with a go at the Basic Obstacle Course and as usual they hit separate showers to get cleaned up before the rest of the day. Josh had a run in the Fun House scheduled for eleven and it was ten till seven when Tina stepped into her shower. She was just lathering up when Josh opened the shower door and stepped in with her.

Other than several long, passionate kisses the only other touching was washing each other. Once rinsed off, Josh picked her up and carried her to bed, sitting her on the edge before kneeling in front of her. She laughed and laid back as he spread her legs and repaid her oral taking of him days before.

When he felt she had been properly dealt with he stood, leaned over and kissed her before walking away, leaving her on the bed with her legs hanging off it and her chest heaving from the excitement of what he had induced in her.

He was standing at the stove, fixing Breakfast Steaks and scrambled eggs when she walked up to him, fully dressed and wrapped an arm around his waist.

"Well Tina, are you relaxed now?" He asked.

"Relaxed isn't the word I would use, but yes, I am. Thank you."

"I have to say it was also my pleasure. Now hold onto those feelings when we get to the Fun House cause we need to move our tactical situation down the road."

"What about our non-tactical situation?"

"Clean the Fun House if you want to find out about that." He said with a chuckle.

They were standing in the corridor at the first door at eleven.

"You ready?" He asked her.

"Yeah, let's do this."

The trick with the Fun House was that there were twenty rooms total. Time started when the first door was opened and ended at the opening of the last door which opened back into the corridor. Each room had four doors and often a target in front of the door. If that target was hit, it would move out of the way via a track cut into the floor so that door could be accessed. Shooters quickly learned if they entered a room with no targets turned to engage, not to accept the room as empty, but watch to see if a target might turn as you are preparing to exit the room.

Josh opened the final door and stepped into the corridor as Tina fired her last shots in the last room as a target did turn on them during the exit phase. When she stepped out of the room, she quickly cleared her pistol and holstered it, then all but jumped into Josh's arms. She had no hits on her body this time and neither did Josh from her lack of taking a target in time.

"All right you two, break it up!" Came the Sergeant Major's voice from behind Josh.

Tina released Josh and planted her feet on the floor as Josh turned in the direction of the Sergeant Major. They waited until the Sergeant Major drew near before Josh spoke.

"So, how'd we do?"

"You know damn well how you did Captain Kramer. Now before you two go back to your bungalow and celebrate, the Colonel wants both of you in her office as soon as you reload. Don't drag your feet, get reloaded and get to the Bunker."

In the Break Room, she pulled Josh's head down and gave him a quick, but passionate kiss, then began refilling her magazines. At first Tina did not understand the rule that no person leaves their quarters without a weapon and full magazines, but one of the explosives instructors told a story of the original commander of the Twenty-First being shot at her desk by a vetted, Government agent that had been assigned to them during an operation.

When they walked into the Colonel's office, Garcia handed them two large envelopes, one for each of them.

"Inside you will find everything you need for identification and travel. The credit cards have a one hundred thousand dollar limit on each of them but use them with caution, or in other words, make sure you need to use them beforehand. Place your actual items in the envelope and return it to me this afternoon. This includes your cell phones. Go by Communications and they will issue you new phones that have been upgraded with new coding, so no one can listen in on our conversations."

She paused for a moment.

"Josh, check out one of the Volvo SUV's and the two of you head for Dallas. You'll find hotel reservations in your envelope. Buy clothing and things you'll need away from here using the credit cards, just make sure you turn in your receipts when you return. You have three nights in Dallas. Have fun. Now get out of here I have work to do."

Once at the bungalow, Josh told Tina to hold off on any thoughts of tearing up the sheets until they get to Dallas. They packaged up their identification and cell phones then went to Communications and checked out their new phones. From there they went to the Bunker and turned in their packets, afterwards the Sergeant Major issued them Sig Arms P938 pistols with four magazines and holsters to carry while out of the compound. Included with the pistols were permits to carry them in Texas.

Josh was changing into civilian clothing when Tina walked in nude with two dresses in her hands.

"Which one?"

Both were modest in cut, but Josh picked out the light blue dress. She tossed the other on the bed and put the one he picked on then smiled.

"Okay, I'm dressed."

"What no panties?"

"Maybe tomorrow, but not today and certainly not tonight."

Josh laughed then took his trousers off and removed his boxers. "There, that better?"

"Oh, hell yes it's better. Now hurry up, Dallas is waiting!"

They had barely entered the hotel room when Tina's dress came flying off and she was dragging him to bed. Even as frantic as it seemed, they took a long time before the final act was played out, leaving both of them almost exhausted on the bed with her lying on top of him.

"Josh, I know what you are thinking, but no, this is not how I dealt with men before. This was me to you and they never discovered this part of me. They were paying for my body, not my soul."

Josh just lay there holding her as she slowly slipped off him to lay snuggled tight to him. After a bit he could tell by her breathing, she had gone to sleep, and he let himself relax and soon followed her.

The time spent in Dallas was like a whirlwind between sexual combat, eating out or room service, and doing the shopping required of them based upon a list of suggestions in their packets, to include matching luggage.

Even though Tina was actually thirty-one, she looked to be in her mid-twenties while Josh was twenty-eight. The cover for them once they set off on their mission were honeymooners, which meant part of their costume was matching wedding bands. The way they tore up the bed, fit that scenario very well.

They spent a lot of time going over their cover with his name being Joshua Hamilton and her maiden name as Katrina Rodriguez utilizing her dark complexion and ability to speak fluent Spanish. His backstory was he had a small construction company in New Mexico and had received a nice insurance settlement after a car accident which explained several of the scars on his body and she was a Legal Secretary whom he met while settling his insurance claim. This gave them the money to tour the world on their honeymoon.

When they returned to the Compound, their luggage was taken into Supply where they slightly abused it to make it look as if it had been roughly handled by airport baggage handlers. Once they had a specific location to be at, tags would be placed on the luggage to show it had been in other locations during their honeymoon.

All they could do now was wait for Intelligence to tell them where to go and what to look for.

Paris

Paris was once the height of glamour for couples to visit but with the Islamic Incursion, the glamour faded nearly to black until the World Monetary Crisis and the French, as with many other countries, forced the invaders out of their country who were nothing more than a drain on the economy. Paris was still repairing the damage done to it decades earlier.

Josh and Tina had a suite at the Le Maison Favart Hotel waiting for them when they arrived to begin their portion of the search for the backers of the Mecca Attack. They only had a name to go on and not much more than that, but for them, it was a start.

An hour after they had checked in, they went out to see the sights and do some shopping. When they returned to the hotel, in the bottom of one of their shopping bags were Sig P938's and silencers along with four magazines each.

It had been ten days since their return from Dallas and sexual interaction between them had moved form being frantic to a casual occurrence as both knew they were together to find the source of over six hundred thousand humans dead at the latest count.

The name they had was of one Paul Renoir, location unknown except he was last known to be in Paris. What Tina wasn't aware of was they were not the only operators from the Twenty-First in Paris. Twenty-four other men and women had entered Paris starting four days before they arrived and were working the leads provided to them by the Intelligence Section of the Twenty-First. Their mission was to locate and watch Renoir until Josh and Tina could make contact with him and hopefully find out who was next in line up the ladder to the top of the sponsors of the attack.

Renoir had been in the Foreign Legion with Luis Ortega, one of the men who executed the Mecca Attack and died from being poisoned. Renoir was also the Legionnaire that had reported Ortega killed in the Congo and that they were not able to recover his body.

The Intelligence Section was working around the clock digging bits and pieces out of the electronic world in an effort to pin down Renoir's location for conformation by people on site.

Josh and Tina played tourist as much as possible trying to stay mobile so if a call or text message alerted them to a location, they could move in on Renoir. It was turning cool in Paris now and this helped them conceal their weapons, but Tina was unhappy that she could not lay by the hotel's pool in the tiny bikini she had bought.

Josh wore a western cut jacket which hid the silenced Sig in its shoulder holster very well, but in a small pocket inside the jacket was a syringe and two vials of the so called truth serum which Tina had been threatened with by Colonel Garcia.

They were having coffee in at a little café when Josh's cell phone buzzed he had a text. All it had was an address of an apartment. They finished their coffee and hailed a cab.

The apartment was a second floor walk-up and Josh took the lead as they slowly moved up the stairs and down the hall to the apartment. He had removed his pistol from the shoulder holster and had it in his front pants pocket with his hand firmly gripping it. This both hid the pistol and gave him quicker access to it if needed.

At the door, Josh put his ear to it in order to detect any sounds but as he leaned back, he looked down and saw that it appeared to have been recently pried open. He stepped back from the door and looked at it carefully as Tina watched the hallway.

Both were wearing flesh tone latex gloves and he carefully reached for the door knob as he brought his pistol out, ready to use.

The door opened without hesitation and Josh entered it quickly, ready for a fight with Tina following closely behind him.

He paused sweeping the main room of the apartment as Tina quietly closed the door then they moved to a hallway. He would check a room while she watched then she would move to the next room as he watched. In the bathroom at the end of the hall, they found Renoir, with his throat cut. From the looks of the blood covering his body, he had been dead for several days.

Josh took several photos with his phone before backing out of the bathroom, then sent them to the Bunker in Texas. When he stepped out of the bathroom he could not find Tina which sent the hairs on the back of his head tingling. Slowly he moved back up the hall, looking into the rooms as he passed until he hear a noise coming from the front of the apartment.

When he entered the main room of the apartment, he found Tina had dumped a waste basket on the dining table and was rummaging through the trash. On the desk in the room, Josh could see the victims laptop lying busted up on it. He ignored Tina as he went to the laptop, set his pistol down within reach then removed a folding tool from his trousers pocket and began taking the computer apart.

It only took minutes to get the hard drive out of the computer and into an anti-static bag he had in his interior jacket pocket. Turning to Tina, she had several things laid off to the side as she began shoving the trash back into the waste basket.

She took the waste basket back into the kitchen and returned with a clean, unused trash bag and carefully placed the items she had taken from the waste basket in it. Tina then sealed the trash bag and shoved it into her shoulder bag before nodding to Josh.

They eased out of the apartment with their pistols in hand ready if needed, then slowly went down the stairs in order not to be caught in the elevator.

Outside, Josh turned left and started walking down the sidewalk after holstering his pistol.

"Tina, give me the trash bag."

Tian pulled the trash bag from her shoulder bag and handed it to him unsure what he was going to do. She watched him remove the anti-static bag from his coat pocket, take a large rubber band from another pocket and wrap the two bags together. A Paris Police car pulled up to the curb in front of him and he walked up to the passenger side and leaned over to talk to the Police Officers, dropping the bags in the lap of the man on the passenger side. He only spoke to them for a moment before moving away, taking Tina's hand and walking away.

"What was that?" Tina asked.

"What do you think it was. Everything we collected will be in Texas as soon as possible."

"How?"

"Not my problem and we're not cleared for that information."

"So we are not alone in this?"

"They are support, it's our operation. Now stay focused."

When the returned to their hotel room, both of them checked for bugs before speaking about the operation.

"Josh, you've always known we had backup, didn't you?"

He reached up to his right ear and carefully pried out the ear bud in it.

"Yes I have. But they are not the only ones out there. Five Mossad agents have been identified trailing us. Now pay attention. Renoir had been spotted and followed back to his apartment. He was being watched but someone got to him before we could get there. I don't think they wasted much time interrogating him as they did killing him, and the apartment certainly was not searched as well as it could have been, so that leaves out both your people and mine."

"Josh, I was not aware of any Mossad agents following us. And that ear bud tells me you have been listening to your people all along. Why didn't you tell me?"

He never spoke to her as he looked at her eyes. She finally lowered her head as she replied for him.

"It's because your people still do not trust me. I guess I can understand that. It's because I'm an unknown."

Josh never answered as he walked over to the room's phone and called room service to order dinner.

Budapest

Two days after they found Renoir's body, Josh rented a car and they drove to Berlin to chase another lead. Tina had withdrawn into herself, dressing in pajamas at night, showering alone even as they slept in the same bed. This didn't bother Josh as he figured things were starting to get too comfortable between them, and they still had a lot of ground to cover before the end was in sight.

Berlin was a waste of a week as every lead they followed came up empty. Tina finally came to him in the shower the fourth night in Berlin, but for only that one night. Josh never considered what they were doing was anything other than sex and took it as it came to him.

Budapest was a different story. They had barely checked into their hotel when there was a knock on their room door. Josh was off to the side with his pistol in hand when Tina answered the door. At the door were two men, one of whom Josh knew, the other was unknown to both him and Tina at that time. Josh told Tina to let them in.

"Terry, what the hell are you doing here and who is this with you?" Josh questioned.

"Josh, the boss sent me and this is Abram, he's Mossad and vetted through the Bunker. Have you scanned the room?"

"Yeah, just finished. Now what's this all about?"

"According to Intelligence, you've been ID'd. No one knows yet how, but there is chatter that the Wizard is on the prowl and people are running for cover."

"Josh, we lost a man last night when one suspect decided to run. He's wounded, but got away with help from others. We tried to stop him without success as you can guess." This came from Abram.

"Who is the suspect?" Josh inquired.

"Heinrich Blumenthal."

"I know him." Uttered Tina.

"How?" Josh Asked.

"Moscow."

Josh just nodded an acceptance of her answer, then turned to Terry.

"What's the plan?"

"We're looking for Blumenthal, both us and the Mossad. Once we find him, the boss wants you to try to take him alive if possible, remove him if necessary."

"Any idea how many are involved?"

"With Blumenthal, there were four others involved in the fire fight." Abram answered.

"Why don't you take him out once you find him?" Tina asked.

"That's our job." Josh answered for Terry.

Terry briefed them on the rest of the information they had at hand with Abram putting in from the Mossad data available. They were to wait at the hotel until a final location could be confirmed, then a team would take them to the site.

Three hours later Josh was contacted to scrub the mission in Budapest as Blumenthal was killed by the Hungarian Border Police when the car he was riding in tried to crash the border into Romania. All four passengers in the vehicle were killed either by gun fire or in the crash. Any information that might be written down or on a flash drive was now in the control of the Hungarians and that would require a political maneuver to retrieve it.

Josh had them change hotels just to be on the safe side since a Mossad agent had knowledge of their location. He had worked with the Mossad before, but he did not know the agent Terry had introduced to him, and he still had doubts about Tina.

It was bothering him that every person they were pointed at were known to Tina from her past, and those people were turning up dead. The strain of not knowing if she was part of the problem or part of the solution was starting to wear on him.

Twenty-four hours later, they were on an airplane back to Texas.

Separation

Arrival in Texas was not without a bit of drama as Josh was taken into the Command Bunker and Tina was taken to one of the bungalows without Josh's luggage which was taken to a different bungalow. When Tina asked about the separation, all she was told was that it was the Colonel's orders.

Josh was sitting in Colonel Garcia's office, waiting as she read a file that she had been going over when he entered the office. He was a patient man and knew that to interrupt her reading would only delay her telling him why they had been brought back to Texas.

She finally finished the file, closed it then looked at him.

"Josh, it seems that someone is listening in on our communications otherwise the word that the Wizard is in action should have never been known. Terry did not know who was point on this operation until after they had linked up with the Mossad and the word was out that you were in the mix."

"How bad am I burned Colonel?"

"The Wizard is being mentioned, but not your name, only that you are a Marine, and there are no photographs of you out there, even a real fuzzy one."

"I guess that is as good as it gets at the moment then. What now?"

"We have teams out all over Europe and the Middle East but information is slow in coming. The Mossad are advising us as they develop information, but they are having more problems than we are having since everyone blames the Israeli's for the attack."

"At the risk of repeating myself, what now Colonel?"

"You're going into isolation for the next forty-eight hours and we are sending Captain Chipovskaya home, back to Israel."

"Reason for sending her home?"

"Several Josh, but we never should have paired you with a partner."

"Colonel say what needs to be said."

"We are concerned she is or will be a distraction."

"Yeah, well she is that for sure, but never on the job, outside the hotel rooms."

"Now your hedging Josh."

"Somethings not right and I can't put my finger on it. For someone who was undercover, playing a prostitute, she has the passion part down pat, even better than she should. She's hiding something and I just can't put a finger on it."

Garcia motioned with her hand for him to give her more.

"Colonel, it seems like every time we key in on someone, she knows him either by the name we are given or another name. All from her time in Moscow."

"Do you think someone is cleaning up behind her? Removing those she slept with just in case someone knows something they shouldn't?" Garcia inquired.

"That's possible, but it still does not explain how my nickname got out there. Something else, see if your Russian contacts can locate and identify the other working girls Tina had contact with."

"Do you think there is a connection?" She asked.

"If there is, sending her home just might get her killed."

"We never considered that. Now what to do with you for a few days?"

Josh put a slight grin on his face before answering.

"Maybe I can think of something."

Garcia frowned.

"If you are thinking about a lovely Texican lady, forget it. Besides having you public as you were the last time you were with her, she has moved on in case you have not been paying attention to the entertainment news."

"No I haven't as you know I stay focused on the job. What happened?"

"Josh, it has been nearly nine months since we pulled you out of her bedroom. Because she has had what we call hard contact with you, anything with her name attached gets flagged. About four months ago she started seeing a director, a Miles Jessup. Last week her agent announced they were engaged."

Josh sat for a moment with a look that Garcia could not read.

"Good for her. I hope he treats her well. So sending me back to the Corps is the only option you have at the moment but I can see that being a problem too if you need me back here on short notice."

"Josh, how about I send you down to the Gulf, to one of our contractors there to work on a shrimper?"

"Fine with me Colonel, when do I leave?"

"As soon as you can pack for that type of work. I'll arrange things after you leave to pack. Anything else?"

"Yeah, one final thought. Button hole Tina and have her give you her clients list, then run the dickens out of it. Don't let her try to tell you she doesn't remember all of them because she is too sharp to forget who did her. Also cross check it with the Mossad. One final thing, get her pimps name and her Mossad contacts name and run them through an MRI to see just how clean they are."

"Sounds good Josh, now go get packed."

"Yes Ma'am."

He was about to open the door to her office and leave when she stopped him.

"Josh, one final thing. I can see putting you and Tina together as we did was a mistake. One we shall not make twice. Do you want to see her before you leave?"

"No Ma'am." He answered then exited her office.

Garcia knew there was still something he was hiding, but decided to let it go as he would say something when the time came. She got on the phone to arrange his being on a shrimper, one of their contract boats to assist handling operations in the Gulf. Ten minutes later it was settled with the boats Captain to arrange living quarters for Josh. Her next call was to the airfield to arrange transportation.

She then called Sergeant Major Gonzales in, and told him to go get Tina and bring her in for a talk.

After Tina had unpacked her things and thought about her being separated from Josh, she started to leave the bungalow to go

94

to the Bunker and find out why they were separated, but looking out the front door window she saw two operators standing on the front porch, both leaning back against the pillars holding up the porch roof, watching the door. She quickly recognized she was in detention, a prisoner without bars to hold her in.

She went to look out the back door and saw the same thing with the men sitting in an ATV. Tina went back to the living room and turned on the television to see if there was something to take up the time as she waited.

Tina was listening to soft jazz on a music channel on the television when there was a hard knock on her door, which actually startled her. She muted the television and went to the door. Opening it she found the Sergeant Major waiting for her.

"Captain Chipovskaya, the Colonel wants to see you. Come with me please and leave your phone."

Tina took her phone from her back pocket and set it on the small table next to the door and passed the Sergeant Major as he stepped aside to allow her to pass. She took a quick look at him to assess his capabilities and saw he was not wearing a standard military pistol rig, but what many considered a competition rig designed for a fast draw and reload.

She knew something about Sergeant Major Gonzales from her Mossad briefing before coming to Texas. He might have been old enough to be her father but was considered by man within the Mossad as dangerous as a pit viper. He was a legend within the Special Operations arena from his time in Delta Force.

When she entered Colonel Garcia's office, she immediately knew that whatever was going to happen, she was not going to be happy with it as Colonel Garcia was on the phone speaking Hebrew, and what Tina heard was not pleasant. She looked behind her to see not only the Sergeant Major blocking the door, but also Garcia's number two on her team, Gunnery Sergeant DeMello.

"Captain Chipovskaya, here."

She looked at Garcia who was now holding the phone out to her. She took it and identified herself. The voice on the other end was curt and told her to cooperate with Garcia then hung up, leaving Tina shaking inside.

Tina handed the phone back to Garcia as she spoke.

"What do you want from me Colonel?"

As Garcia exchanged the phone for a note pad, she responded.

"Sit and write down the names of your Moscow clients, the other working girls you might had associated with, anyone who you kept company with during your tour in Moscow. This includes those you just picked up in a bar for a one night stand. Make sure you add your pimps name, and the name of your Mossad contacts."

"Colonel, I have already given you those?"

"No, I don't think so. Now I do not expect you to remember everyone's complete names, but give us a name. In case it hasn't dawned on you, it seems everyone we have attempted to get too has died, and they all have one thing in common at this point. And that is you."

Tina sat down and started to write then stopped.
"Colonel, when will I be able to see Josh again."

"Josh is packing for a new mission and will leave within the hour. So you will not be seeing him before he leaves."

Tina started to ask where Josh was going but stopped knowing she would not be told any more than she had already been told. She began writing the names that were easy for her to remember, even putting the names down she knew were already dead.

As Tina was remaking her list, Josh was loading his car for the trip to Galveston and the mission to get away for a time. Every time he thought of Tina he got an itch in the back of his neck he could not get past. He took a look towards the Bunker, then drove away with that itch still bothering him.

While Tina was doing as ordered, Gloria was watching her monitor as Bricker was sending her the names of pimps and prostitutes in Moscow that had turned up dead over the past eighteen months. To the side was a map of Moscow showing Tina's known residences plus the location of each dead pimp or prostitutes residence for the same time frame as hacked from the Moscow Police computers.

Gloria just motioned to the Sergeant Major to enter then close the door which he did so quietly that Tina never noticed what was going on behind her. He just leaned back against the door waiting to either escort Tina back to her bungalow or kill her if need be to protect Gloria. What he did not know was that Gloria had her Sig pistol lying in her lap if she needed it quick.

Tina completed her list of names and handed it across to Gloria. Gloria compared that list to the list Bricker had posted, then selected one name and pulled up the photo of the person it was connected too. It was the photo of a modestly attractive blond prostitute and according to the data; she shared the same apartment building with Tina. Gloria turned the monitor to where Tina could see the photo without having to move to see it.

"How well did you know this girl?" Gloria asked.

"We partied together several times? If a client wanted more than one girl to service him, either she contacted me or I contacted her. We also partied with other girls and clients in group parties."

"Did you ever party alone, just the two of you?"

Tina hesitated before answering.

"Yes, she and I have shared a bed with just us, no men involved. We also shared a female client. You'll find her name on the list."

"Captain, she's dead. Bullet in the brain."

"That's a shame. She was just trying to survive."

"Hers is the only name on the list you gave me, but I'm going to run some photos by you, if you know them by a different name which you have listed, tell me. If you know them but did not list them, also tell me and tell me why they were not listed."

"Yes Ma'am."

As Tina responded no to a photograph, Gloria moved it to a separate folder. If she recognized a photo but the name on it was different from what she had written down, she told Gloria. A couple she said she had seen several times but never knew their names.

It took over an hour to process through the photographs with roughly a third of them going into the known file. Once they had that complete, she sent the known file back to Gunner Bricker to run a deeper back ground into each one as possible. Along with that was the names which Tina could not connect with a photograph, also for further examination.

"Captain Chipovskaya, you will turn over your weapons and communications to the Sergeant Major. He will move you from the bungalow to one of the rooms down in the tunnel and a guard will be posted on your door. The Sergeant Major will also inspect your luggage for anything which might be used as a weapon. Do you understand my orders?"

"Am I under arrest?"

"No, at this moment you are in protective custody. Someone is out there removing your history and I do not want you in any position to join that group."

"If I'm not being arrested then why removed my weapons?"

Gloria looked at her for a moment before Tina responded to her look.

"It's because I'm also a suspect, isn't it? Alright Colonel I'll play the game, but what about the Mossad? What will you tell them?"

"As little as possible, especially since your pimp and Mossad contact in Moscow are still alive as of this morning. Now why is that when all others, including foreigners have been murdered? Then there is the knowledge of the Wizard being involved in now two operations without him every leaving a calling card or this command broadcasting his involvement in those operations?"

"I have no answers Colonel to those questions."

Gloria switched to Hebrew as she continued speaking to Tina.

"Josh would have left you in Europe, in a trash bin if he suspected you were working for the other side, so I take his concerns seriously about you. You are part of the problem we are facing but to be honest, I do not know exactly where in that problem you lie. Until then I have to protect my assets and this command, and will do so regardless whose toes I step on."

"I understand Colonel." Tina replied in Hebrew.

"Sergeant Major see to my instructions."

"Yes Colonel. Captain Chipovskaya, if you will."

What Gloria was truly concerned about was if they had a mole within the Group. One that had ties to whomever was behind the deaths in Moscow and the virus that was now running rampant in Egypt.

Galveston

Tina was taken to a door within the Bunker that led to a stairway leading down into what was commonly known as The Tunnels. This was the actual barrack, living quarters for the full time personnel working for the Twenty-First.

But they were not alone in this walk to her new quarters as a female Air Force Master Sergeant named Watkins led the way with the Sergeant Major behind Tina. They walked down one corridor, then turned right down another then left down another until they came to the end of the corridor and what Tina figured was her guard standing next to a door with her luggage at his feet.

Once in the room, Tina was told to stand on the other side of the bed from Sergeant Watkins as she opened each of Tina's luggage and carefully removed each item, laying them on the bed in a manner as not to mess them up any more than they already were.

Everything was gone through to insure Tina did not have something stashed inside some article of clothing or her personal bath items. Once her luggage was gone through, Tina laid everything from her pockets onto the bed then Watkins frisked her to determine if she was hiding anything at all.

When they left, they took the luggage telling Tina it would be returned after it was x-rayed. All she could do at this point was to try to get comfortable and wait out whatever was going to happen to her. She put her things in the rooms dresser, changed into comfortable clothing and just sat in the only chair in the room and waited.

Within an hour Tina heard a knock on her door then the lock being worked. The door opened a few inches and she heard a females voice.

"Are you decent?"

"Yes, come on in." Tina replied.

The person entering was dark wearing a white uniform and an apron which showed signs of usage. In her hands she had a tray of food and she just came over to where a small table was sitting and placed it on it. Once in place she turned to Tina.

"I'm Chief Wingate, the Senior Mess Steward for the Hospital's kitchen. On the tray you find our buffet menu for the next week, breakfast, lunch, and dinner. Notate what you wish to eat for each meal and that is what will be brought to you. Orders from the Bunker is that no special order food, it all has to come off the buffet to prevent anyone from tampering with it. In case you are wondering why I opened the door without waiting for you to tell me to enter is because these rooms are sound proof to allow couples to enjoy themselves without bothering their neighbors. We'll serve you off the prepared line at 0700, 1200, and 1700 hours. If you wish something late, call the kitchen and we'll advise what is on the line and you can pick from there. Are there any questions Captain?"

"No, thank you for the food and information."

"Captain, in case no one told you, if you select channel 419 on the television, you'll see a list of books contained within our humble library. When you select a book on the television, it'll give you a basic synopsis of the book so you can decide if you wish to read it. The book will be brought to you when the next chow delivery is made."

"Thank you again Chief, I was wondering how to spend my time in jail here."

"Captain, believe me, you are not in jail or even a holding cell. Those have a narrow bunk with no mattress, no television, and the toilet is out in the open along with no shower. From my understanding of your situation is that the Command Staff are doing everything they can to insure your protection."

"Thank you Chief but it certainly does not feel that way."

Wingate just nodded and left the room so Tina could eat. When she looked at the tray she noticed that the flatware was metal, which any trained operator worth their rations would know how to make into a viable weapon. She set the menu off to the side and dug into the Shrimp Salad that had been delivered to her.

After she ate, she used the facilities then decided to see what the television could provide to kill the time. She was amazed at the number of channels, both broadcast and internet she had available. She chuckled when she discovered the porn channels available without restrictions and just to kill a minute or two, she scanned the contents until she fell upon a channel which interested her.

The channel was listed as Russian Gang Bang and when she opened it, there were thumbnail photos for each video. One caught her eye and she opened it and viewed in for about thirty seconds before she hit pause on the control then moved close to the television and examined it closely.

Tina quickly moved to the phone on the nightstand and saw a laminated note taped to the nightstand saying this was a restricted phone and only gave the numbers to the kitchen, and medical. She punched in medical and it was answered in two rings.

She explained who she was and told the female on the other end to contact Colonel Garcia and have her contact her, and that it was an emergency. She was told to hold, then what seemed like forever Colonel Garcia answered.

"Yes Captain, what is the emergency?"

"Colonel, this is going to sound crazy but I found a video on your television network that you really need to see before someone else discovers it and takes it off the net."

"We'll be right there." Garcia hung up the phone.

It seemed forever before Tina heard the door unlock and Colonel Garcia along with the Sergeant Major entered the room. Tina just pointed to the television. Gloria walked over to the television and looked at the frozen scene on it then looked at Tina.

"Yes Colonel, that's me but what's important is the men. I never knew their names but they all spoke Spanish."

Gloria stepped out of the room and picked up the wall mounted phone where her guard was standing and dialed three numbers. Tina had no idea whom she was talking too but heard Gloria instruct the other person to locate and download the video Tina on her television.

When she walked back into the room Gloria noticed the Sergeant Major leaning in close while running his finger across the screen.

"What are you thinking Sergeant Major?" Gloria asked.

"Hidden camera, close circuit TV type. Captain Chipovskaya, during your activities, were you aware some were being taped?"

"No Sergeant Major I was not. And before anyone asks, this was not my contract, I was asked to join by Svetlana, the blond. Also I said they spoke Spanish, but it was not their first language as their speech patterns were often hesitant, as if looking for the right word."

Gloria stood quietly for a moment then gave orders as she was looking at the monitor.

"Sergeant Major, take her up to Intelligence, find her a desk and let's see if there are other videos out there we should be looking at. I'll get with Gunner Bricker and have him begin running facial recognition on the players. Tina, if it is not too personal, why were you looking at porn?"

"Colonel, after what I have experienced, most of the porn everyone thinks is so great is comedy to me. I get no desires or excitement from watching it, but I often get a good laugh."

Gloria just nodded her head then turned for the door. The Sergeant Major indicated for Tina to follow.

As this was playing out at the Twenty-First, Josh was pulling into the parking lot at the docks where he was to meet up with shrimper he would be working with during this time away from operations. Or so he thought.

Standing at the gate to the docks was a familiar face belonging to one retired Chief Boatswains Mate Pablo Cortez. Pablo had a grin on his face as Josh walked up, offering his hand in greeting.

"Pablo ya old goat, how are things with you?"

"Fine my friend, life is good. Let's grab your things and get to the boat. We are shoving off as soon as we get your things stowed away."

As they were walking back to Josh's SUV, the conversation continued.

"I thought I was getting an apartment and it'd be a few days before we went out?" Questioned Josh.

"You know how it is, Change Twelve to Paragraph One of the orders." Pablo answered.

"Shrimping or something else?"

"Something else. Let's get your gear aboard and one free from the dock, you can read the package."

"Alright. By the way, how is the family?"

"They are good. You know Amelia turned eighteen."

Josh never looked at Pablo.

"Pablo, she is still too young for me, but you have one very attractive girl there.

Pablo laughed. "Yes, she is and it has been a thorn in my side with her being chased by half the boys and many men in the area. Thank God she has a good head on her shoulders, but she still has the hots for you."

"Pablo, currently my cut-off age for females is twenty-two. And it increases every year. Besides, she is your daughter and I'd never touch the daughter of a friend."

"I know my friend, I was just pulling your chain some. Let's get away from here and we can talk more over a cold one about the package."

"I'm traveling light Pablo."

"No problem. Everything you might need is aboard the Consuela."

"Why do I have the feeling I was not told everything before I left the Compound?"

"Ah, sounds like Garcia is playing games again. We'll know more once you open the package."

Once clear of the docks and all the greetings of the deck hands was complete, Josh went below to the small dining area and opened the package sitting on the table.

After Pablo navigated the Consuela out into the Gulf, he came below as his First Mate piloted the boat. He found Josh just shaking his head.

"What's wrong Josh?"

"I'm supposed to go ashore near Scarborough on Tobago, meet up with a Valkyrie team and do away with a small time drug dealer. But here is the kicker. I'm supposed to get myself killed in the process so the Valkyries can report my death."

"Sounds like Garcia is going to make you a ghost."

"Sounds like it. The operation I have been working on has glitches. My face might not be known, but the word in the Intelligence community is that the Wizard is on the prowl."

"That's not good Josh, not good at all. This Tobago mission sounds like it is designed to keep you in play while making the world think you are dead."

"Yeah, that it does. Anyway, let's get this taken apart and see what we need to do."

As the Consuela changed course and headed for the island of Tobago, Tina and a select crew were going through hours of porn looking for every film she might have been in. She knew the location of the group sex orgy and Gunner Bricker was ripping through layers of computers, hacking data to locate the actual owner of the apartment.

Facial recognition was working to identify the men in the apartment, especially once it was shown that more than one camera was operating, giving wide views of the sexual activity.

No one spoke to Tina about her actions within the apartment and focused just on the unknowns including the third female which Tina said was the only time she had interacted with her. Svetlana was one of the dead hookers already listed, and they needed to find out about the other female as quickly as possible.

Gunner Bricker overheard two of his technicians talking about one of the hookers looking like the unknown individual working at one of the desks. He went to Colonel Garcia with the light gossip. Gloria calmly left her office and stepped upon the Sergeant Major's desk to over look the Bunker Floor which surprised the Sergeant Major as he was working on a file at the time.

"Listen up people!" Gloria got everyone's attention. "Everyone knows the rules we have in place concerning both male and female operators from having sexual contact with potential targets or their support personnel to gain intelligence. The CIA, MI-5, the Mossad and the rest of the intelligence world does not have those restrictions."

"What most of you are not aware of is that several of the females in the videos that are being examined have turned up with a bullet in their brain. It doesn't matter what name you wish to apply to those women for doing what they are doing in those videos, what matters is they are humans who have been murdered to keep a secret that they are suspected of knowing in relation to the attack on Mecca."

"One of those women is a Mossad agent that was working undercover, gathering intelligence concerning a different operation. I cannot fathom the courage it takes to enter into such an undercover situation knowing that each day could be their last."

"What many here do not know is that during General Conley's reign as commander of the Twenty-First, she had a female operator that went rogue in a fashion when she discovered an invaluable source of intelligence during the Insurrection which could not have been gathered except for violating orders and taking the target to bed. For over three months that agent provided sex and companionship, each day knowing she could be discovered as she was able to get information out to one of the Tiger Teams."

Gloria let that settle in for a moment.

"Once the Insurrection was over and the agent recovered she was on the verge of suicide from the fear, the terror she lived with daily knowing what would happen to her if she was caught stealing documents and other items needed by General Conley to prosecute the war. Her efforts shortened the Insurrection and saved hundreds of lives."

"Intelligence operations is a nasty business and thankfully we do not play by the same rules the others play by."

"So if I hear a single derogatory bit of gossip concerning who might be in the videos we are examining, that individual will find themselves running the Master Course in their underwear until I get tired of watching them. Do I make myself clear here people?"

There was a resounding "Yes Ma'am" from the room.

"Good, get back to work so maybe we can solve this puzzle."

Tina sat and felt as if the undercurrent within the room she had been feeling was lifted from her shoulders. She went back to work looking for specific videos that might have her in it. As she was going through the videos she also thought about what Colonel Garcia had said and wondered why she never had the feelings of fear that the female Garcia had mentioned. She put it out of her mind and for a second wondered what Josh was up too.

Tobago

Pablo put Josh ashore utilizing the Zodiac on the Consuela where he met up with Suzette from the Valkyrie team already on the island. As soon as they were out of sight, Suzette grabbed Josh and planted a hot, wet kiss on him. When they came up for air she spoke first.

"Damn Josh it is good to see you again."

Josh chuckled. "Yeah, I can tell, but we don't have time for this right now."

"I know Josh. Anyway, it'll take about forty-five minutes to get you into position, then if the target keeps his schedule about another hour wait."

"That'll give me time to shift position if I don't like the one you ladies picked out for me. Let's get this done."

His target tonight was a native of the island who dealt with prostitution and drugs but had recently moved into gun smuggling and sex trafficking of minor females. The package on him showed he had half the police in the district on his payroll and the ones that were not were afraid to deal with him due to the last honest cop being discovered washed up on the beach with a bullet in his brain.

The target operated out of a bar in a two story building on the outskirts of Scarborough with the second floor functioning as a brothel even though it was listed as rooms for rent.

Suzette took him to a low building, a single story approximately two hundred meters from the entrance of the bar with a ladder leaned up against the back of it. Josh climbed up onto the roof and took a hard look at the layout. He had a clear shot down the street and onto the old sidewalk in front of the bar.

From this position his modified M4 silenced carbine would have no trouble taking the target down. The custom loaded 7.62x39 Russian cartridges were perfect for such a mission and the expended cartridges would eject out onto the street instead of bouncing around on the tin roof he was lying on. All he had to do was wait for the queue from inside the bar that the target was leaving.

Suzette informed Josh that Porsha, one of her team had a job in the bar as a waitress and would let them know when the target was leaving. Porsha would make her exit out the back door once she alerted him via a single, long tone on his radio. All he had to do now was wait.

Once Josh was settled in and double checked the range with his range finder, he insured he was ready to go then relaxed. The problem with having to wait for a target was it gave him too much time to think.

Suzette had kissed him again before he climbed upon the roof and he could still taste her raspberry lip gloss. They had spent three days together before he left for Samoa, and the memory of those days were still fresh in his mind. She was an animal in or out of bed, but she was also adamant that it was just sex, no more, no less, and it certainly wasn't less.

Then there was Delores and her easy going approach to sexual combat. She knew what she wanted and worked hard at it once engaged, but otherwise it seemed that it did not matter the rest of the time.

But Tina bothered her still. There was something missing in the equation he could not lay his hands on. Nothing was off limits to her which probably came from working undercover as a prostitute where there, nothing was off limits. Still, where was she involved as far as the Mecca attack was concerned? Was she an innocent bystander or a player? Was the sex an attempt to distract

112

him or was it a way for her to try and remove the memories of long, cold Moscow nights tending to the desires of clients?

His thoughts shifted to the mission in front of him. Any operator within the Twenty-First could deal with the target but why him? He knew that Colonel Garcia had a thing about sex traffickers, especially when minors were involved. She had never turned down a mission involving sex traffickers when it was feasible, but again, why him.

Suddenly his earbud buzzed with the tone advising him the target was exiting the bar. He was in position when the first body guard exited with the target close behind him. Right behind the target was his other bodyguard. There was a loud noise to Josh's right and the target looked in that direction. Josh felt the trigger break as he sent a one hundred and twenty-four grain hollow point bullet downrange. As he recoiled back into a firing position, his trigger finger relaxed enough to allow the trigger to reset, and as the targets head was exploding from the first round entering his left eye socket, Josh slightly elevated and fired a second round into the chest of his bodyguard standing behind him. It was a redundant shot as the first bullet had traveled through the targets head and impacted the bodyguard in his right lung.

Josh shifted to the left and caught a solid sight picture on the first bodyguards head as he was turning to see what was happening behind him and placed a bullet behind his right ear. He did not wait to see the results and he began moving off the roof. At the back edge, he stood then just stepped off the roof having already checked the ground before climbing the ladder.

He dropped his night vision goggles down over his eyes and could see Suzette standing back in the brush. She was waving to him to hurry. Just as he met up with her, three shots came from behind him. As he was turning to face an aggressor, she grabbed his arm.

"Ignore it Josh, he's on our side. Now let's go!"

What Josh was not aware of, Suzette had sprinkled fresh blood on a bush where she was standing. They moved through the underbrush to her car, then she drove away as if nothing was happening.

"Suzette, what was that all about back there?"

"That was one of the good guys, one of the good cops for this district. He's the one who made the noise to get the targets attention. He'll report he saw you leave the top of the building and fired on you, but did not pursue since he was afraid you'd kill him. Tomorrow they'll search the area and find blood I sprinkled on a bush. Didn't Garcia tell you the plan?"

"Not that part. What more is there she left out?"

"Pablo will give you that part once you meet up for extraction."

Suzette headed North, cutting across the island then followed the coastal road towards the Northern part of Tobago. Josh pulled his map of the island and using a red lensed penlight kept track of where they were by the signs along the road.

A few kilometers past Mount Dillon, she stopped at a small stream which according to Josh's map, lead to the ocean. Suzette leaned over and gave him a quick kiss.

"Josh, follow this stream to the beach. Pablo will meet you there. I'll go on up to Charlotteville and meet up with my team. We have a fishing charter waiting on us to take us to Miami. From there we go to the Compound. Maybe I'll get lucky and see you there."

Josh never commented as he got out of the car and slipped down off the road into the stream where he stood allowing his eyes to become accustomed to the night before utilizing his night vision

114

goggles to move down the stream. He was pissed that he had not been fully briefed.

He took his time moving downstream since nothing had gone as he was used too, except the target engagement. Why did Colonel Garcia have a plan inside of a plan without advising him of such so he would be prepared?

The closer Josh came to the coast, the slower he progressed until at the edge of his night vision, he could see Pablo kneeling next to the Zodiac up in the wide mouth of the steam.

Josh keyed his radio and spoke a single word. "Biscuits."

"Gravy" came back as Pablo gave him the all-clear, but Josh was still nervous about how things were going. Josh took a deep breath and started towards Pablo, almost expecting a bullet with each step.

Pablo was bent over the side of the Zodiac when Josh moved to it and looked up at Josh.

"Give me a hand, this is running longer than computed."

Josh looked into the Zodiac to see what Pablo was doing and saw a body in the bottom dressed as he was dressed.

"What's going on Pablo?"

"Give me a hand damnit. This is your body. As of tonight, the Wizard is dead. Move it Marine, we need to get out of here."

Josh slung his carbine behind his back and reached into the Zodiac and helped Pablo pull the body from the boat.

"Don't let his feet drag the ground and let's move upstream a few meters." Pablo instructed.

They moved the body about five meters upstream then Pablo moved into the stream and lowered the body into the water. He then removed a bag from his leg pouch, cut it open and began to pour blood out of it on the body and into the water. This had an immediate reaction of drawing crabs towards the body.

Pablo motioned towards the Zodiac, and together they pushed it back downstream until they found deeper water then boarded the boat. Neither spoke as Pablo navigated the boat the rest of the way into the ocean then turned it towards where the Consuela was waiting for them.

When they were well out to sea, Josh finally spoke up.

"Pablo what the hell is going on?"

"What do you mean what's going on? Didn't Garcia brief you on this?"

"No, not a word."

"Damn that woman. Playing games again, but I'm sure she had her reasons. That body belongs to a small time hood from Detroit that caught a couple of rounds in his back a week ago. He's been kept on ice until we thawed him out while you were doing your thing. By daylight, the crabs should make him almost unrecognizable and once we get back to the Consuela, I'll send a report saying you never arrived at the pick up point and we had zero radio contact with you."

Josh sat for a moment before replying.

"So Garcia makes an announcement that I'm missing in action then when the body is discovered, the world will think that the police officer who fired the shots after I cleared my roost and found his target in the darkness."

"Josh, from what I was told, you have been burned, and this will be a way to be reborn if necessary."

"Pablo, it could also be a way to find the leak in the works. The only person to learn who I am outside of the Group saw me in a beard, long hair, and glasses. Correction, another has seen me without the beard."

Neither man spoke again until they met up with the Consuela and got the Zodiac tied down forward of the pilot house.

"What do we do now Pablo?" Josh asked.

"We drop our seines and go to work. No way can we go back into port with empty holds. Get cleaned up and stow your things then get some rest. In the morning we should be off Key West and we'll see if we can snatch up some shrimp."

Return to Port

Both men were wrong about Garcia or anyone within the Twenty-First announcing the death of the Wizard. To do so would have acknowledged that he was in fact one of their operators. What did happen over the next few days was the news coverage out of Tobago concerning the deaths of the target and his bodyguards, then the discovery of the body in the stream.

Josh learned via the news that a truck had been stolen and then wrecked near the point he was dropped off and the interior was covered in blood. Maria, one of Suzette's team had stolen the truck and was nearly an hour behind Suzette with it. She drove it off into the ditch, then sprinkled blood on the drivers seat, floorboard and door before being picked up by Porsha and Carmelita to meet up with Suzette at the boat taking them off the island.

Since Josh preferred the modified M4 platform utilizing the 7.62x39 round from the Kalashnikov AK-47, and one was found in the stream, equipped with a silencer and the ammunition found in the weapon matched the empty cartridges found during the murder investigation, the Tobago authorities claimed that the infamous Wizard who was known for dozens of deaths in Central and South America had finally met his end at the hands of one of their policemen.

It took nine days for the Consuela to reach port with a decent catch. During that time events within the Bunker had accelerated with Tina giving the address of the apartment used in the orgy, and a team already in Russia moving on it.

As the Consuela was being tied to the dock, Colonel Garcia made an appearance, then boarded the craft once it was secure. Garcia, Josh and Pablo went below decks to the mess area as the other hands prepared to off load their catch. Josh was still upset about not being advised of the entire operation.

"Colonel Garcia, I'm sure you had your reasons for leaving things out of my brief, but I damn near killed that policeman when he fired those shots as part of the plan. If Suzette had not been as close as she was and grabbed my arm, there would most likely be a dead policeman to add to my resume."

"Josh, that was a last minute addition, one we were not sure of until you were committed."

"Alright but Suzette could have warned me, or did you not consider that?"

"Captain Kramer, I understand you are pissed but be careful of your tone."

Josh just looked at Garcia knowing if he spoke again, she would rake his ass over the coals. He stood up, went to the coffee pot and poured a cup before sitting back down.

"Josh, here is an update for you. Captain Chipovskaya located a video of her in her Mossad operation which has led us to others, unknown to us. The apartment is in a building belonging to Viktor Tereshkova and from what we have learned it was used by him to entertain guests during their visit to Moscow."

"Entertain as in providing hookers for his guests?"

"Exactly. Captain Chipovskaya claims to have no knowledge of those activities being filmed and in fact they are all over the internet including over a dozen she was not involved in. From our people in Moscow right now, it seems the building manager had placed hidden cameras in the apartment once he was aware of its purpose and was making a tidy sum selling the edited videos out to porn sites."

"Good God, I bet that made her feel just wonderful having people in the bunker observing her undercover activities. So where does that put her at this time?"

"We're still not sure. One videos of her with five men and two other females is of great interest to us. When I left the Bunker we had identified three of the men, all educated in Bio-chemistry, and all of Muslim heritage."

Josh sat for a moment thinking.

"Tereshkova has the money to fund the attack on Mecca, but I find it difficult to believe Muslim scientists would go along with such a thing considering it was Mecca."

"Here is another thing Josh. Tereshkova is a Russian Jew although very few people are aware of that fact."

Josh took a drink of his coffee as he thought about that information.

"Why would a Russian Jew want a major war in the Middle East?" Pablo finally spoke up with the question.

"Gunner Bricker is hacking him right now, trying to dig out every financial transaction to see if he can find a reason. We find it hard to believe he would do such a thing simply because he is a Jew knowing that Israel is boxed in the way they are. Tensions are climbing over there and the death count is still soaring. The President has quietly moved two fleets into the Mediterranean and ordered the Pacific fleet into the Persian Gulf to reinforce the forces already there."

"Anything else?" Josh asked.

"Only that the men we have identified on the video have disappeared off the planet."

"Shark bait by now." Pablo chipped in.

"Most likely." Josh added. "So back to what's now?"

"Are you up to going to Russia?"

"Yes but with a caveat. Tina stays in Texas."

"Care to explain why?"

"Something is still not right with her and I do not want to be looking over my shoulder all of the time."

"Fair enough then. Let me get back to the Bunker and make the arrangements. You stay here until then."

Colonel Garcia left the boat, leaving Josh and Pablo to help with the offloading. Josh told Pablo he'd stay on the boat so there was no need to get an apartment and he certainly wasn't going to stay with him as long as Amelia was in the house. Pablo started to laugh at that comment then stopped recognizing that Amelia would attempt to crawl into Josh's bed if he was there.

Since Josh had nothing better to do than sit around, he told Pablo that he would take care of some of the boat's maintenance while waiting for the call from Garcia so the crew could get some time off instead of spending that time working on the boat. Pablo gave him a short list of things to accomplish and left Josh to himself.

Josh was cleaning the windows of the pilot house when he looked down the slips to see a woman watching him from four slips over. She was wearing cut-off jeans and a bikini top. She waved at Josh and he was polite in returning it then went back to work.

It was nearly two hours later the female was standing on the dock next to the Consuela with two bottles of beer in her hand.

"Hello, my name is Lori and as hard as you have been working, I thought a friendly cold one would fit in nicely."

Josh looked at the woman judging her to be in her late forties, maybe early fifties, well fit, tanned, with large nipples pushing out of her bikini top.

"Hello Lori, my name is Josh. Thanks for the offer."

She smiled, stepped on the boats gunnel then dropped down onto the aft deck. She offered Josh a bottle and just smiled at him.

"Well Josh, it looks as if you are a new member of Pablo's crew."

"Yeah, I hired on the day we put out to sea. Is that your boat down there?"

"Yes, I run a fishing charter. Are you staying on the boat?"

"Yeah, Pablo is considering putting back out in a few days and I've yet to get an apartment since hitting town."

"Well, I have a couple of ribeye's needing cooked so I'll give you a holler later unless you have other plans."

"No other plans Lori. You call and I'll haul my butt over."

She laughed as she stepped back up on the gunnel then onto the dock. Josh figured he knew what she was wanting for dessert, and three hours later he was in the forward cabin of her boat giving her what she desired.

The next morning Josh was sitting on the aft deck of the Consuela along with Pablo drinking coffee when Lori walked by and waved at them with a sly grin on her face. Pablo lightly chuckled and waited until she was out of hearing before he spoke.

"Lori is a widow and it looks like she has her eye on you Josh."

"Yeah, well you should have warned me about her."

"Should have? Let me guess, you have already seen her tan line."

"What tan line?"

Pablo had to spit out the coffee he had just taken as he laughed at what Josh had said. Nothing more was said about the widow living four slips away. That night she invited him for a repeat performance.

The next morning Josh was working on the Port Boom when his cell phone pinged with a text. He was to meet with a C-17 at Ellington Joint Reserve Base at 1700 hours for transport South. Josh acknowledged the text, ran the math in his head and decided he had time to finish what he was doing. A C-17 and going South meant he had a mission.

Pablo showed up about thirty minutes later and helped Josh finish working on the boom then helped him pack his gear, double checking his weapons. As they were loading his things into his SUV, Lori pulled in a few parking spaces down from them and walked over to them. She told Josh she had lobster for dinner and he apologized that he had received a call from his mother that his father had fallen off a ladder and was in the hospital in Phoenix, and he was heading back home to be of help until he was released. Lori told him maybe another time and just left as she came.

Pablo looked at Josh and only smiled.

"What are you smiling at Pablo?"

"Lori goes through men like shit through a goose but it seems she has a weak spot for you."

Josh looked over where Lori was taking shopping bags from her car then back to Pablo.

"She needs to find a good man to take care of."

"Maybe she thought she found one?"

"Drop it Pablo. It was entertaining but she needs someone closer to her own age. Well that's it, I need to get out of here. You take care Pablo."

Pablo offered his hand. "Watch your ass Marine."

South Bound

When Josh boarded the C-17 at Ellington, he was surprised to see Colonel Garcia and her entire Orchid Team, dressed for action. She waved him over to her, and handed him a briefing package as the aircraft began to roll.

The short end of the briefing was that they were going to jump into the Santa Cruz District of Argentina to check out an abandoned research facility that had been funded by Viktor Tereshkova. Reports they had received was it was abandoned at the same time the attack on Mecca.

Josh had trained and worked with the Orchids before, so he had no problem joining them nor they having him along. The mission concept was simple in that they were going to enter the facility, find what they could about it then leave without causing too many problems if possible. Any and all guards would be Tased and bound if possible as they did not wish to leave bodies behind.

After some thought, Josh pointed out whether they left alive guards or bodies, Tereshkova was bound to be notified within hours of discovery of those facts.

As Josh was rereading the brief to insure he had everything, Gunny DeMello, the Number Two on the Orchid team sat a duffle at Josh's feet. Josh looked up at DeMello.

"Captain change out your upper. That 7.62x39 is your trademark and you are supposed to be dead. Pecos built you a new upper in five-five-six and it's true out to three hundred meters. He said for you to load your own mags then put all the 7.62 stuff back in the duffle."

Josh stripped his vest and ammo pouches of his former life and loaded the new magazines after he changed out the upper on his M4 platform. He checked the balance of it, sighting down the aircrafts cargo bay and found that Pecos had came real close to duplicating his former upper on the weapon.

Once that was done, he just leaned back and dozed off until time to suit up for the HALO drop into Argentina. By treaty, the Air Force could overfly Argentina, but had to maintain a minimum of thirty thousand feet in doing so, this required a High Altitude jump with a Low Altitude Opening aka HALO. At that altitude, oxygen masks were required.

Josh always got a kick out of people asking him how many jumps he had under his belt when they saw his Parachutist Wings. Not because he thought the actual question was funny, but because you don't actually jump from a plane, you step out of it, especially off the rear ramp of a C-17.

Because he had the point on this mission, he was the first out into the darkness and into cloud covering. Jumping into clouds was a high risk situation because you had no horizon, even in the dark to align yourself too.

There was supposed to be an infrared beacon on the ground, placed there by CIA Operator to locate the actual Drop Zone, but communications was sparse, and Josh knew that trust between the Twenty-First and the CIA was not always as it should be.

Josh broke through the clouds at about seventeen thousand feet and immediately saw the beacon with his night vision goggles. At twelve thousand feet, he pulled his small drogue chute to slow his descent as he adjusted his attitude towards the beacon. At four thousand feet, he pulled his main chute, checked it once, then began guiding himself towards the beacon. His small mission pack was high on his chest and his rifle attached to his right side, so there was no drop bag to deploy prior to landing.

The hard part of a night landing is judging where the ground is actually at through the night vision goggles, plus he could tell it was a grassy plain they were jumping into but not the

126

depth of the grass. He was about thirty feet to the right of the beacon when he pulled hard on his risers to nearly stop his descent and gently touched down finding the grass was barely knee high.

Josh never looked to see how those behind him were doing as he quickly gathered his chute into a ball. He walked over to the beacon, removed his parachute harness, and dropped it all next to the beacon. Next came his oxygen mask as the small oxygen tank was attached to his harness.

As he was getting his pack transferred from his from his front to his back, the others walked to the beacon and dropped their unneeded gear and got themselves ready to move out. Looking around he had six people with him which meant the entire Orchid team was on the ground and safe.

They were approximately fifty kilometers from Puerto Coig in the extreme South of Argentina. Josh pulled his GPS unit that already had the location of the target facility logged into it, and pulled up the bearing he had to take to reach the facility approximately three kilometers away. He had seen the lights of the facility during the descent, and had noticed it was barely lit up.

He looked one more time at the team with him and asked a single question.

"Everyone ready?"

He heard Colonel Garcia tell him 'go', and he headed in the direction of the facility. There was a stand of trees between the landing zone and the facility but a faint glow of lights over it helped guide him to his target.

As he was nearing the tree line, he heard a vehicle behind them and turned to see a truck enter the field with its lights off. That had to be the CIA moving to retrieve the beacon and the gear they left behind. He waited for a moment to watch the vehicle to insure it was not following them, then saw Garcia who was right behind him wave him forward.

Josh slowly picked his way through the stand of trees which at the far tree line brought him to within four hundred meters of the security fence of the facility if he had judged the distance correctly. He paused to get a good view of the facility then pushed his goggles up, out of the way to give his eyes some rest.

At that distance, the facility was fairly lit up so he could see if there was a guard walking around the perimeter. Garcia moved up beside him.

"What do you think?"

"It would nice if we knew more about this place, especially guard rotations and such, but it is what it is. Give me a few more minutes as my eyes adjust then I'll go take a look. Spread out along the tree line and give me cover as I move forward."

Josh had to smile to himself as he was giving orders to one, a Lieutenant Colonel, then second, the Black Orchid herself. But she knew, understood what was happening since he was on point for this mission.

A few minutes later he moved out without speaking to Garcia and even though he was hooked to the others via radio, he never heard a word as he trusted her to deploy the others as specified. He also knew that he had one of the best snipers in the world at his back watching the area for him as he slowly made his way towards the fence.

One advantage he had was the grass outside the fence had not been mowed, giving him cover if needed instead of being exposed in a bare strip of ground as it should have been. This told Josh that either it was planned to make it look completely abandoned to the casual observer, or the people responsible for guarding the place were too lazy to deal with it.

At the fence, he checked with a volt meter to see if the fence was wired, electrified. Zero voltage then he looked for any small wires which if broken would set off an alarm. The grass was shorter inside the fence yet it still looked to be needing mowed. He took one last looked around then stood up for a moment to see if there was a beaten path around the building as if a guards walked around it at night. He could not see a path so he squatted back down, pulled a set of wire cutters and went to work on the fence.

Every place he cut, he checked to see if there was a thin wire he had missed until he had cut a hole in the fence wide enough to crawl through without worry of hanging up on it. He broke an infrared Chemical light and hung it above the opening for the others to guide on.

Josh entered the compound and quickly moved to where he could see the front entrance. He pulled an eight powered monocular from his vest and looked at the gate shack just inside the main gate and could see two heads above the short wall through the glass. There was a sudden glow telling Josh one of the men was lighting a cigarette or cigar. The only other light was from a small desk lamp to the front of the shack.

His earbud popped, then he heard Garcia.

"We're at the fence."

He pushed his talk button on his radio twice to let her know he received her message. It was roughly seventy-five meters to the guard shack and he just waited for about fifteen minutes to see if anyone else popped up, or it was just those two men as he also figured out how to cover the distance between his location and the shack.

Josh keyed his radio.

129

"One, come forward." Instructing Garcia to move to his location as he watched the guards. It took less than a minute before she was behind him, concealed from the guards by the building.

"What do you think?" She whispered.

"Taser please." He reached his hand back to her without taking his eyes off the guard shack. He felt her place the Taser pistol in his hand then without saying another word, he moved in a direct line towards the shack.

Two guards and he only had one Taser which would not work too well once at the shack. He moved quickly with his rifle up and ready if needed but once he knew he could take the shack door, he slung the rifle behind his back, drew his own Taser and kicked the door without pausing. Both men never had time to react before Josh hit them both with Tasers.

As soon as he kicked the door, he heard Garcia give the move order and the team flowed into the compound with her moving to support Josh. He moved more into the shack allowing Garcia to enter as he held the men with the Tasers providing jolts of electricity from moment to moment to prevent them from being able to defend themselves or attack him.

Garcia moved to the nearest man and as Josh released the Taser, she moved the guard onto his belly and secured his arms with nylon restraints, then gagged him. She moved to the second guard and did the same. Once secured that way, Josh joined her and tied the men's ankles together so they could not stand up. Josh stepped on the cigar that was burning near an overflowing trashcan.

They waited until two of the Orchid's had made a complete circuit of the building, checking for any other guards. Once completed, they went to the front doors of the building to see it was wired with a keypad security system.

Sam Clements, the Orchids commo man moved to the door and began working on the keypad. It took nearly ten minutes before they had a green light on the pad and they heard the doors unlock.

Before entering, each individual put on a respirator, to prevent inhaling any toxicity inside the building. Every room had to be checked and every file cabinet, every desk drawer inspected as they moved through the building and time was not in favor of a prolonged search.

There were no signs on the door or above them to advise them what was in them as they each took a room. Anything they felt was of value was laid on top of any desk of flat surface to retrieve as they backed out of the building. The only person not in the building was Bill Hendricks, the team sniper who was still in the tree line watching over them.

Every person had a small, electric screwdriver with interchangeable tips and every computer found was taken apart, and the hard drive removed them placed in an anti-static bag. These were placed in their packs.

But it was inside the laboratory they hit gold. Dozens of photos were taken of the lab along with samples collected by swiping the surfaces with sterile pads and then sealed in plastic bags. It was through a door at the back of the lab they found a replica of the device used to release the virus on Mecca. Photos were taken of it from every angle possible.

In the lab, they found test tubes which had not been cleaned, which they took, also placing them in sterile, sealed bags. As photos were being taken of the device, DeMello opened what appeared to be a walk-in freezer and notified Garcia she need to look at what he had found.

Inside the freezer were eight bodies and being that the building was under power, they were frozen. All were dead with a bullet to the brain. Frost was brushed off them as best it could be and photos taken. Fingerprints were useless since the fingers were frozen and the grooves of the prints filled in with frost.

As they were about to leave the freezer, Josh moved to the bodies, removed his wire cutters and cut the right thumbs off each body, handing them to Garcia who understood what he was doing and placed each thumb in a sterile bag. Once thawed out, the thumb would give them both a print and DNA.

They moved out of the building gathering the things stacked on the desks until their packs were stuffed. Now the question arose of what to do with the guards.

Garcia only took a minute before telling her people to move the guards into the freezer. She stood alone in the freezer and put a bullet into each man's head, then closed the freezer.

Once everyone was out of the building, the keypad was reset and the security system was back in operation. At the hole in the fence, DeMello helped Josh replace the portion he had cut out and zip-tied it back together so at a distance it would not look like it had been cut.

Before they removed their respirators, each person was sprayed with a disinfectant to destroy any of the virus which might have gather on their clothing while inside the lab.

They moved to the main gate and loaded into the two vehicles that belonged to the guards and headed west, for the border with Chile. They crossed the border just after daylight at a place where there was no border guards and stopped at a location already predetermined in the mission profile. Garcia made a cell phone call and then the team moved out to another location to

132

await pick up by a Marine Osprey from a carried off the coast of Chile.

And hour later they were airborne. They were taken directly to a Fleet Carried and boarded a COD, a Carried On-Board Delivery aircraft and flown to a Chilean Air Force Base South of Santiago, where they boarded the very C-17 that had dropped them into Argentina. Their packs went into sealed shipping containers to preserve the items inside and once done, everyone just stretched out on the web seats along the fuselage and went to sleep.

Texas Again

Upon landing at the compound of the Twenty-First, everyone, including the flight crew of the C-17 was taken to the Group's hospital to be checked for possible contamination with the virus while the interior of the C-17 was sprayed with a strong disinfectant.

Once the blood work came back negative on the C-17 crew, they left to return to their home base. Each transport case was opened in the sterile environment, with every item checked to insure no contamination was present before moving the papers and computer hard drives to Intelligence to deal with.

The removed thumbs had thawed enough a print was taken of each then tissue samples for DNA. Those items were entered into the computers and a search began on them to determine the ownership of each individual if possible.

When Josh had his blood taken for testing, he also advised them he had sexual relations off the Compound which meant it also had to be checked for any manner of social disease before he was allowed to engage any female on base as per protocol. He came back clean.

As he was gathering his gear, Garcia came to him.

"Josh, do you wish to see Tina?"

"No Colonel, and if possible, she should not know I was here."

"What's going on with you two?"

"Colonel, something isn't right and I can't place my finger on it. It has nothing to do with what she did in Moscow for the Mossad, but I keep getting this feeling we are being played."

134

"You think she is directly involved with Tereshkova?"

"I don't know." Josh replied.

"We've found no direct connection with her to him as of yet, but our team in Moscow has recovered hours of video taken by the building manager which never made it too the internet. If Tereshkova was screwing her, it's a good chance it's on one of those videos."

"It could be one or more of those bodies we found are also in the videos and Tereshkova is trying to clean up loose ends. But for a man who has made a fortune not making mistakes, leaving that facility intact, and the bodies in the freezer was a stupid mistake on his part."

"Well here is something the public does not know. Tereshkova's father was KGB. Tereshkova is actually his mother's maiden name. Those folks tend to be a bit over confident."

"Colonel, I'm going to go get some rest. DeMello said my SUV was brought up from Ellington so I'm going to shower, change and go to Waco, get a motel room and hide there until you need me."

"Alright Josh. Hopefully we'll have something for you soon."

As he was picking up his gear he spoke again without looking at Garcia.

"Ya know what Colonel, I starting to think I would like to just go back to being a simple Marine."

"Once this is over, I think we can arrange that."

"Thanks Colonel."

Josh showered and changed in one of the Hospital's Guest rooms, the headed for Waco where he got a motel room and just sat, leaned back on the bed and played roulette with the television remote until he found a movie that he could tolerate while waiting.

As he was eating Tex-Mex for dinner at one of the local restaurants, the plane bringing the Moscow team and over one hundred hours of video landed at the Compound. The Conference Room had been set up with eight computers for those viewing the videos in order that no one could look over their shoulders for what DeMello called a cheap thrill.

The concept for checking the videos was simple in layout. Each video was to be viewed at the lowest, fast-forward speed to determine if the following people are on that disk. Viktor Tereshkova, Captain Chipovskaya, the five men in the orgy video.

While they were in Argentina, three of the men had been tentatively identified via facial recognition. Two were Iranians and one was a Palestinian based upon passport photos. It was hoped the thumbprints and DNA would confirm their identities along with the other men in the video plus the men in the freezer. The men who had been identified were reported to have been educated in England with degrees in Bio-Chemistry.

When any of the aforementioned individuals were identified on a disk, the time stamp for that disk would be notated along with the individual for further examination once all disks were scanned. At that time they would be slowed down to their normal speed and the audio would be recorded also for further examination.

Tina Chipovskaya was located on three of the disks, but never with Tereshkova and never within an hour of his appearance on the disk. It was noticed that he would meet with whomever was also in the video then upwards to an hour later she would appear and service that individual either in the main room or the bedroom which was also bugged.

Once audited, the videos were to be broken down with screen captures of each individual which was sent to facial recognition to try to get a fix on the people Tereshkova was doing business with.

Since Josh had nothing better to do as he waited for the call, he did what he often did, went to the nearest public library and sat while reading. He was well into the book he had chosen when a familiar voice quietly spoke in front of him.

"What 'ca reading?"

He looked over the top of the book to see a pair of brown legs exposed beneath a knee length, print dress. Josh looked up to see Suzette standing in front of him. Suzette was from New Orleans, a Creole with the body of a fashion model and modest looks.

"Agatha Christie's Death On The Nile."

"That seems appropriate all things considered."

"What are you doing here Suzette?"

"I have a few days before I have to report back to Norfolk, and I thought we might be able to spend that time together, unless you have a better offer."

Josh closed the book, stood and just smiled at Suzette. She followed him as he returned the book to the shelf he had taken it from, then wrapped her arms around his neck and kissed him. An hour later he had her pinned to the bed with her arms above her head, holding them in place, but even though his manner of pinning her down was pleasurable, he wasn't doing a thing to increase the pleasure.

"What are you doing Josh, get moving?"

"Suzette, first you are going to tell me how many people are on me, watching me."

Suzette knew that if she wanted more than him just resting inside of her, she had to answer him.

"Two teams, one Valkyrie, the other an Ops team. They've merged to make it look like couples out and about. Garcia is concerned about your safety."

"And your purpose here?"

"My purpose here is to be in the position I'm in at the moment, and that was my only thinking. But you can get off me now because the moment has passed."

Josh moved off her as she lightly groaned with his withdrawal from her, and sat up on the side of the bed. Suzette moved off the bed and went into the bathroom to clean herself. She returned to where her clothes were lying and began getting dressed.

"Josh, this was my last mission, the last time we would see each other and you just ruined it. Are you hung up on that Mossad chick?"

"Yes, but not how you are thinking."

"You know, if you had asked me about your coverage while we were undressing or afterwards, I would have told you. But to do what you just did was cruel as far as I'm concerned. What's happened to you Josh?"

He just sat and tried to find an answer for her, but the words never came to mind.

"Josh, when I asked Garcia where you were and why, she told me you were thinking about getting out of this business. I think you are right as it is turning you into something you are not. Now pay attention to me. I'm returning to Norfolk and to a man who if things goes right, I just might let him have me, and I'm not talking about for a night or weekend. I'm tired of this also, plus I'm on the list for full Commander. Goodbye Josh."

She gathered up her purse and left him to his own thoughts. He knew he had screwed the pooch with Suzette something terribly and did not know how to make it right with her, even if it was over between them. Josh went to shower to get her stickiness from his crotch and the smell of her perfume off his body.

Afterwards he just lay on the bed in a pair of sweat pants thinking that this mission was as fouled up as anything he had ever seen. He was silently praying that it did not kill him before it was over.

It was nearly an hour after Suzette left that there was a knock on his door. He had his Sig 938 in his hand when he looked out the security peephole to see Suzette standing, waiting for him to open the door. When he did, she just walked in and once he closed the door and turned to her, she slapped him hard enough to knock him back against the door.

"You son of a bitch! I swear to God if you ever pull a stunt like that on me again, I'll cut your dick off and hang it over my bed to remind future lovers to not fuck with me!"

Josh could taste blood in his mouth from her slap causing him to bite the inside of his cheek.

"I'm sorry Suzette, I really am. This operation has me paranoid. Did you just come back to take your anger out on me for being a jerk?"

"No, you stupid bastard, I came back because as much as it pains me, I wanted to spend this time with you."

"Why Suzette?"

"Shut up and enjoy the time, or tell me to leave, take your pick."

Josh stepped to her and pulled her close as he kissed her. She leaned back once the kiss was broken and ran her tongue across her lips.

"You're bleeding."

"Now you shut up and get out of those clothes." He softly spoke to her.

As Josh and Suzette were recovering from a second attempt to find Nirvana, at the Bunker, Air Force Technical Sergeant Robert Winslow hit pay dirt with Disk Number Seventeen. This was the disk that the orgy had originated from and it started with Tereshkova meeting with the five men before him leaving, then Tina and the other females arriving to entertain them approximately twenty minutes later.

Colonel Garcia stood behind Winslow as he scanned the disk again, advising him to just fast forward through the sex portion to see what might be at the end of the disk. What she was wanting to see was how things were dealt with after the men had expended themselves from their lust.

The reason for this was that at the beginning, two men entered with Tereshkova and acted as interpreters for Tereshkova since he did not speak Persian when dealing with the men from Iran or Urdu to the men from Pakistan. Early in the video, it was discovered all five men spoke English, but never spoke it around Tereshkova or the females.

What Garcia was silently excited about was that one of the men with Tereshkova had earlier been identified as Tina Chipovskaya's Mossad handler, known to her as Abiyram Rosner, who had seemed to fall off the face of the earth soon after Tina had been recalled to Tel Aviv. The other man would have to wait for an identification.

After the party, the unknown man came back to the apartment and collected Tina and Svetlana, leaving the other blond female alone in the apartment since the men had left to other accommodations. Garcia watched to time clock on the video to see how long it would take before the other female was collected.

Roughly fifteen minutes later, Rosner returned to the apartment, opened his pants and had the female perform oral sex on him before taking her from the apartment. This female had not showed up in the files they had hacked concerning murdered or accidental deaths of prostitutes, but this had Garcia wondering what if she was not a regular prostitute, but one that worked from time to time in the business as she attended to another profession or even a student.

Garcia instructed Gunner Bricker to not only search all police death records for the girl, but to expand out to other cites not covered by the Moscow Police District.

As Garcia was starting to leave the Conference room after giving her instructions, Air Force Master Chief Karen Watkins, Bricker's number two asked to speak with in private. Garcia just motioned her to follow and they went to Garcia's office, closing the door behind them.

"Alright Karen, what's up?" Garcia asked.

"Colonel this may sound strange coming from me, but how can a woman like Captain Chipovskaya, allow herself to be treated as she was working undercover like that? I mean I understand how

141

a prostitute does it, but she is no whore, prostitute if you get my meaning Ma'am."

"I can't answer that Karen, only Captain Chipovskaya can do that. But it has to take a toll on her, and you know the reason we do not allow our operators to engage in sex with their targets or the targets associates."

"Yes Ma'am, I actually feel sorry for the Captain, having to put herself out that way to gain intelligence when how many time she just took it deep without any gain, if you understand my meaning."

"I understand Karen. But she's not the first nor the last woman working within the Intelligence Community that has gone in that direction in hopes they can gain vital intelligence. But I can say that the greatest fear they have to deal with is discovery. Only the good Lord knows how many women have died at the hands of those they were spying on from the bedroom. But now we have something else we need to consider here. The darker man in the video Winslow discovered who was translating for Tereshkova was also Chipovskaya's Mossad handler. From the video, it seems he avoided her, which could have several meanings. Now we have to discover those meanings and move on with this operation."

Karen sat for a moment before responding.

"Colonel, you know I speak Russian, and are you aware that the intent of those men creating the super-virus was to use it against Israel?"

"I caught that from what little Persian I know. Tereshkova double crossed the scientists and once all the data from our trip to Argentina comes to light, we'll most likely identify those five men as being in the freezer. Facial is still stripping the frost from their faces to match them up."

"Thank you for the time Colonel, I'd best get back to work."

"Karen, let me ask you a personal question. Isn't Josh Kramer one of your regulars?"

Karen smiled at the Colonel, then just left the room leaving the question unanswered. Garcia knew that of all the women on base, Karen Watkins was very selective of whom she slept with, and never jumped into a bed without knowing her partner more so than others.

Garcia knew that Suzette and Josh were together in Waco, that she had left in a huff then later returned to his room. Suzette would be heading back to her unit at Norfolk and there was no need to recall Josh at this time. But it was time to introduce Chipovskaya to the new information to see her reaction.

There was one last thing Garcia wanted done and that was to bring the building manager in along with the hard drives from his computers just in case there was something on them not on a separate disk.

She stepped out of office and told the Sergeant Major to have the team sitting on the building manager to bring him in with his computer hard drives.

Garcia left to have an early dinner with her son before she might be called back to the Bunker. She was amazed that the building manager had managed to escape notice for his activities as long as he had. Chipovskaya said she was just bored when she stumbled upon the initial video that had brought them to this point. But now Garcia was getting the same feelings that Josh tried to express that something about Chipovskaya was not right.

Back to Work

Josh watched as Suzette drove away from the motel thinking they had three days without interruption which had surprised him. It had not been three days of passion, eating delivery while nude on the bed, it had been three days almost like being a long term couple playing tourist in Waco, with the time spent on the sheets as long time lovers once they got past the initial making up after Josh's miscalculation with Suzette.

Suzette was three years older than Josh but her Creole heritage made her look years younger. She was educated at Louisiana State before entering the Navy as an Intelligence officer. Her dark complexion, accents and ability to speak several versions of Creole made her almost the perfect intelligence officer to work in the Caribbean.

When Josh finally got around to asking her if she was serious about leaving the Group, she told him she was officially gone once she reported back to Norfolk. And she had not lied to him about the man she was returning too. He was also a Navy Officer, a Doctor, and no, they had not slept together in the short time they had been dating.

She left him thinking about life, her life and his when just before they separated as they stood by her car was that he was the last man she had slept with, and had not been with a man in that situation since. It dawned on Josh that had been nearly two years ago in her room down in the Tunnels at the Compound.

Her car was still in sight when his cell phone announced a text. Opening it up, it was his recall notice to return to the Compound and to duty. Josh loaded his things back into his SUV, and headed back to work.

Tina stood behind Tech Sergeant Wilcox and watched the meeting part of the video taken prior to her and the others entering to entertain the men in it. A written transcript of what was being

144

said scrolled across the bottom of the screen. Colonel Garcia was standing off to the side, watching Tina as she viewed her Mossad handler dealing with the men for Tereshkova. She appeared calm except for a slight tremble in her hands.

Once that portion was complete, the orgy scene had been removed then the scene where Rosner returned for the girl referenced as Inga gave him the blow job. Garcia could not detect any reaction to Tina observing that part of the video. When completed Tina just stood looking at the blank screen until Garcia spoke to her.

"Captain Chipovskaya, at the risk of repeating myself, this is the only time you met or saw this Natalia?"

"Yes Colonel, that was the only time. But there are hundreds, maybe thousands of women in the Moscow area who sell themselves when needing extra money."

"Facial recognition has given us something on her. She was reported missing from Saint Petersburg eight years ago at the age of fourteen."

Tina looked at the photo which came up on the monitor.

"Yes, eight years to be raped, trained, then put to work making some pimp comfortable while she does the work for her money on her back. Do you have anything else on her?"

"Nothing. It seems that she has faded off into the woodwork."

"Colonel, have you talked to Tel Aviv about Rosner?"

"No."

"Unless Rosner or another has Natalia tucked away someplace, you'll never find her body. Part of me is praying

Rosner was just doing his part in an undercover assignment, but I have to be honest with myself in that he has gone rogue. What have you found out about the other man?"

"At the moment, he is a bit of a mystery man. What can you tell us about him?"

"The only thing I know about him is that whenever I was to attend to a client in that apartment, he picked me up and took me home. He never touched me or attempted to use me in any fashion. I don't think he spoke more than a dozen words to me during those times. But from listening to him speak on the video, may I suggest you contact Tel Aviv and see what they have on him. He has a slight accent I cannot put my finger on at the moment."

"Captain Chipovskaya, the reason we have not contacted Tel Aviv is we do not know who to trust anymore. If this is a rogue Mossad operation, who is involved, and who is not? There is no doubt Tereshkova is the money behind the operation, but there are still too many loose ends to contend with. The individual who filmed the events within that apartment will be here in a few hours as we have gotten him out of Russia along with the computer hard drives. Maybe he can tell us more when he gets here."

"Colonel, can I talk to you in your office?"

Garcia motioned for Tina to lead the way as they went to Garcia's office. Once the door was closed and both seated, Tina started the conversation.

"Colonel Garcia. I believe I mentioned earlier that I had slept with Rosner although that was not the name he was using when dealing with me. Now let me add to my earlier statement concerning my mission to Moscow. Do you have a recorder someplace so that you can get all of my statement?"

Garcia removed a small digital recorder from her desk, activated it and sat it so it would pick up their voices.

"I was recruited by Colonel Chofetz of the Mossad for this assignment. The official purpose of the investigation was to see if we could confirm an attempt on the State of Israel utilizing chemical weapons. The truth is that it was felt there were in fact rogue agents working against the best interests of the country."

"Tina, I know Colonel Chofetz, but why you? Why did he pick you?" Garcia asked.

Tina squirmed in her seat.

"I had just finished my basic training in the IDF when I was raped. I wasn't a virgin by any standards, but it was still a rape. But unlike many females who have been raped, I did not withdraw into myself, shunning men. Just to opposite in fact. Once out of the hospital I found it easier to give myself as if something inside of me needed that contact maybe to prove what had happened to me was purely an accident. Before I had gotten too deep into my perversions, I was recruited into the Mossad."

Tina paused for a moment.

"One of the hardest things for a woman to do, a normal woman that is, is to give themselves to an unknown man without thought, especially when their true purpose is to learn about that individual while servicing them. A normal prostitute turns off their minds and just goes through the steps to insure their client is pleased then moves on to the next one. There is something wrong with me in that if your Sergeant Major walked in and opened his pants, I'd let him take me right on your desk without pause. The Mossad quietly nurtured that fault in my personality and used it to their benefit."

"What about Captain Kramer?" Garcia asked.

"Yes, Josh. He's the exception to the rule if you consider it. So what now Colonel?"

"We wait. Captain Kramer has been recalled but until he says otherwise, the two of you will stay separated."

"I understand Colonel. One other thing in case I did not mention it. Even before the world learned of the attack on Mecca, I received a phone call, then a text giving me a single code word which advised me to exit Russia as quickly as possible, and return to Israel. The voice on the phone was female and they only spoke that one word. An hour later I was on the train to Berlin, then a plane to Tel Aviv. I had no contact with Rosner or anyone else during that time."

"What happened when you returned to Tel Aviv?" Garcia inquired of Tina.

"I was debriefed, then tucked away until Chofetz sent me here."

"I think I need to have a long talk with Chofetz then. If there is nothing else Captain Chipovskaya, return to your quarters."

Garcia sat for a long time thinking before placing a call to Tel Aviv. The call lasted for nearly an hour and was very productive in that Garcia was able to send Chofetz a photo of the unknown man to him and he immediately responded with knowledge of who he was or once was.

The man was a Ukrainian Jew named Fedir Balanchuk, who immigrated to Israel with his parents and eventually entered the Mossad after superior service in the Israeli Defense Force. He had terminated his service with the Mossad about five years ago then showed up again as Tereshkova's body guard. Without checking the records, Chofetz had no knowledge if Balanchuk and Rosner had ever worked together. It was also noted that Rosner

148

had not responded to the recall notice and his location was unknown.

Josh reported in and just moved his things into a bungalow until he was given a mission. He was told Tina was being held in isolation for her own protection which Josh just acknowledged as a good idea.

The problem for the Command Staff of the Twenty-First was what to do next.

Decision Time

Video taken from the hard drives after they arrived in Texas gave the more information concerning Tereshkova and his body guards. Tereshkova liked young girls, the younger the better and he was caught on video raping several with Balanchuk and Rosner also raping them later. The building manager said he could not put those out on the internet, but held onto them in case he needed insurance against Tereshkova.

The problem that the Twenty-First was facing, that concerned General Grainger and Colonel Garcia was how do deal with Tereshkova considering his actual participation in the attack on Mecca.

Under normal circumstances, a team would go in and take him out, leaving bodies behind and in this case documentation showing why. But this involved too many countries and Tereshkova was a billionaire.

Josh had examined the information of Tereshkova's estate outside of Moscow for hours and determined it could be taken based upon the intelligence received. But he was honest in that it could be a costly endeavor. His data was double checked by the Sergeant Major and Gunny DeMello who both agreed with Josh's estimate of the situation.

General Grainger ordered a package on Tereshkova to include the rapes of several young girls to be delivered to every Embassy in Washington. She determined at this point it was a political problem, and a law enforcement problem, and could not take it forward to have him sanctioned.

Copies of documents from the computers and files obtained in Argentina, plus the photos of the men in the freezer were included in the package with photos of the prototype dispenser in the garage bay.

The packages were in depth and left no doubt that Tereshkova was the mind and money behind the attack on Mecca. His reasons were still unknown but that was for a court to determine.

The identity of Balanchuk and Rosner was made with the conclusion they were rogue agents, not acting on orders from Tel Aviv. There was a conclusion that Balanchuk and/or Rosner were the ones dealing with cleaning up behind Tereshkova given their pasts.

Since there was no proof, the murders of Svetlana and others were not mentioned in the package.

The packages were built in a near sterile environment so no fingerprints or DNA could be transferred to them at time of construction. The delivery of the packages would be handled by a messenger service in Washington.

It would only take hours before the outcry was being heard all over Washington concerning Tereshkova with the phone lines to the Russian Embassy becoming overloaded with calls.

When the Russian State Police went after Tereshkova, both Balanchuk and Rosner were killed in a gun battle, and Tereshkova took his own life before he could be arrested.

Not counting the people killed who might have given him away, Tereshkova was considered responsible for over two million deaths from the virus which had finally ran its course. There was never a final determination why Tereshkova did what he did as all of his personal records were destroyed by him before he took his own life.

The building manager was given a new identity and immigration status with a warning not to attempt any other manner of expanding his income other than the job provided for him.

Josh and Tina had stayed separated during this time and once it appeared the world was back on balance, he knocked on her door. Their meeting in her room with the door left open was short.

"Tina, you cannot go back to Israel since too many people know of your contact with Rosner. Arrangements have been made to give you immigration status here under a new identity. One thing I want you to do for me and that is to seek help for whatever problems you are having."

"Colonel Garcia didn't tell you my problems?" She asked.

"No, she didn't but I know you are troubled. Seek help and move on with life. Maybe find a good man and settle down."

"I thought I had found a good man."

"No Tina, I'm not the man for you. It would never work."

She just nodded her head and walked into her bathroom. Josh took that as a hint it was time to leave.

From Tina's quarters he went to his SUV with orders in hand to the Second Raider Battalion at Camp Lejeune, North Carolina. He had turned in everything he had been issued by the Twenty-First and was leaving the Compound for the last time.

In the month he had returned to the Compound, he had not interacted with a single female in a sexual manner. He was just glad to have it all over with.

So We Meet Again

Josh had been in command of Golf Company for nearly seven months and he finally felt he had found his true place in the Marines. During this time he stayed focused on running the company and had not taken any time to search out comfort between the sheets. The company was rebuilding after taking a beating in Nigeria even if they had came out on top of the fight, and he was replacing the Company Commander who had been killed in the fight.

Within the Marine Corps is a manner of moving paperwork around called Guard Mail. It is nothing more than a large envelope with a block to place an address and once delivered, the address can be marked through and the next block used until all blocks are filled then the envelope is tossed into the trash. It is big enough to hold legal size notebook paper but the one that was placed on Josh's desk by his clerk looked empty until he dumped it out.

From the envelope came a three by five card with a single line written on it.

"Officers Club at 1930 hours."

He asked his clerk how he obtained the envelope and his clerk only told him it was in their distribution box at Battalion when he checked it after lunch.

At 1930 hours, Josh was standing in the lobby of the Officer's Club trying to determine which room to check out first when he heard a familiar voice behind him.

"I think dinner first, then maybe the bar unless you have a better idea."

He turned to see Suzette in her Navy uniform with a smile on her face.

"Suzette, what are you doing here?"

"I'm on leave and I came to see if I should let my enlistment run out or reenlist."

"Why come here to make that decision?"

"God Josh, for someone who is worldly and can make tactical decisions on the run, you can be dense at times."

"I thought you had a doctor on the hook?"

"The line broke. I couldn't commit to him."

"And you think you can commit to me?"

"Or maybe I need to be committed. Josh shall we talk over dinner?"

They took a small table far from the juke box so they would not have to speak very loud to each other. The waitress was there even before Josh took his chair after being a gentleman in assisting Suzette to set down. She ordered a white wine and he ordered a draught beer. Neither spoke until the waitress returned with their drinks and menus.

"Alright Suzette, what went wrong?"

She took a sip of wine then took a deep breath before responding.

"Four days after I left you in Waco, I fell into Kenneth's bed. I wasn't expecting much, I just wanted to get you out of my system. Of course the first time a couple merge in such a manner there is a learning curve on what each other prefers and enjoys. We slept together several times before we finally had a weekend off together. It was better as he did try hard and I was finally relaxing with him."

She took another sip of wine, then the waitress returned to take their order. Suzette ordered a seafood salad with Josh ordering a Taco salad.

"Okay Suzette, where is this heading?"

"I ended up moving in with Kenneth about six weeks after I returned to Norfolk."

She took another sip of the wine, this time even a larger sip. Suzette sat the glass down and began to fidget with it as she just sat looking at the glass. Josh reached over and gently grasped her hand.

"Again, what went wrong?"

"Last week he asked me to marry him."

"Okay now I'm confused." Josh responded to her comment.

"The week before Kenneth asked me to marry him, Pete DeMello stopped by and handed off my severance package from the Group."

"Yeah, he came by and gave me mine. That was on Thursday, I think."

"Yes Josh is was on Thursday. He brought mine to me also. Anyway, I asked him to lunch but he said he had to get down here to deliver yours. So I asked him where you was assigned and he told me. Until then, I thought you were gone from my life."

"Pete never said he had seen you."

"That's Pete but to continue, I went home that night and tried to once more remove you from my thoughts. Then on Monday Kenneth asked me to marry him."

"You said that already, about him asking you to marry him. Care to cut to the chase here."

"I told him no because there was no excitement in our relationship. And for him being an OB/GYN, he never found the right buttons to really set me off like you could."

"Suzette there is more to any relationship than sex."

"I know that Josh, but to be honest, even if DeMello had not shown up and told me you were here, I would have told him no anyway."

"Why?" He asked thinking he already knew the answer.

"Because I didn't love him and honestly never could."

"Why not?"

"God damn you Joshua Kramer, you know damn good and well why."

"Tell me anyway."

"Because I have loved you since Lagos."

"Why have you waited this long to say something?"

"I thought it was obvious when I returned to you in Waco after that stunt you pulled on me."

"As I look back at that situation, I'm still unsure I can find the words to apologize for that mistake."

"You don't have to apologize because you certainly made up for it before dinner that day."

"Why didn't you say something instead of just leaving me standing in the parking lot watching you drive away?"

"Because I didn't feel we could have more that those short days. You know what, I started crying before I ever left the parking lot and cried all the way to Dallas."

Before Josh could respond, their waitress brought their salads. He waited until the waitress had left them alone again. Neither began eating as both just picked at their salads with their forks.

"Suzette as I remember it, we had no physical contact during the Lagos mission. I think it was about two weeks later that you asked me to take you to bed when we met at the canteen."

Suzette smiled as she looked at her salad.

"We met three times working as your support and each time you intrigued me. Then when we had to extract you cause you were all busted up, you showed more concern for my team than your own self. You refused to take anything for the pain you were in until you knew we were all safe. Honestly I think I had a school girl infatuation with you, but it wasn't until you made love to me the first time I knew my feelings were real."

"You said that you were on leave. How long do you have?"

"Forty-seven days terminal leave if I do not reenlist."

Josh finally took a bit of his salad causing Suzette to follow suit. They ate for several minutes without speaking before Josh continued with a question.

157

"Have you considered where you are staying while down here?" Josh asked her.

"I've taken a room in transit quarters, why?" She replied

"Finish eating then go change into civvies while I go back to my BOQ (Bachelor Officer's Quarters) and then we'll get a room in town tonight and talk about why you are here."

She nearly threw her fork at him as she slammed it down on the table.

"Haven't you heard a word I said? I'm in love with you, what more do you want to hear from me?"

"I want to hear what you expect from me during your time here besides me making love to you nightly."

"Joshua, if I want to just get laid tonight, I can walk over to the bar and arrange that within minutes. Making love to you is fun, but that's not why I am here."

"Then tell me what I need to say that will prevent you from going across the lobby to the bar."

"I don't expect you to tell me that you love me, not tonight, but only that there is a chance for such words."

"Suzette of all the women I've been with, I have stronger feelings for you than any woman. Being in the trade I was in, I took sex as it came and never looked back, but I always looked forward to being with you. I've always had a soft spot for you."

Suzette took a drink of her wine before responding.

"Joshua, you have forty days to decide if you feel about me enough that I let my enlistment expire so I can stay close to you. If not, I reenlist and ask for any assignment as far from you as possible."

"Finish eating then we'll see if dessert is worth your trip down here from Norfolk."

Suzette pushed her salad away, took a final drink from her wine, then stood up.

"Off your ass Marine."

Josh laughed.

"Yes Ma'am Commander Ma'am."

Two weeks later Josh and Suzette leased an apartment off base so they would have more privacy as they learned more about each other away from the bed.

One thing Josh quickly learned was how short a fuse Suzette could have and often lit the fuse just to see how far he could push her before kissing her and calming her down. Once she figured out what he was doing, she would drag him into the bedroom where they had agreed never to take any disagreement beyond the bedroom door.

He spent a week in the field with his company during a training exercise, but took her to New York City the weekend afterwards just to see the sights and be together.

Their fortieth day was a Sunday and as she had tried to pry an answer from Josh during the previous week, he always seemed to deflect giving her an answer about their future. Suzette woke up to the smell of Josh fixing their breakfast. They had been sleeping nude but she put on one of his t-shirts before going in to join him for breakfast.

Suzette gave him a quick kiss as he was fixing scrambled eggs then poured a cup of coffee and sat down at the small kitchen table. When Josh set her plate in from of her, sitting on top of her eggs was a diamond engagement ring. She picked it up and looked at Josh leaning against the kitchen counter smiling at her.

"Quit smiling you bastard. I was going to pack my things up after breakfast because I figured you could never take the one step I've been praying for since we came together."

"Suzette, I'm not going to beg you to accept that ring, it is for you to decide as I only want you happy."

She held the ring out to him.

"Bring your ass over here Marine and put it on my finger."

Josh set his coffee down and did as she instructed. She pulled him tight and kissed him. As the kiss turned passionate, Josh moved her breakfast out of the way, picked her up and set her on the table, then sat down in her chair. Suzette laughed and laid back on the table.

They were married two weeks later after she had returned to Norfolk to be processed out of the Navy. The wedding took place in the Base Chapel with Josh's company officers and senior NCO's holding up an arch of swords.

Before the wedding, Josh made Suzette promise to wait a minimum of three years before considering children as she would still be young enough to have several.

Josh deployed twice with the Raiders, then they moved him back to the regular Marines as first a Battalion Operations Officer, then as a Battalion Executive Officer before he would retire as a Lieutenant Colonel after a successful command of a regular Marine Infantry Battalion that included a deployment to Chile.

They settled near his parents outside Casa Grande, Arizona to finish raising their five children.

About The Author

Leon Michaels is the author of several novels and short stories that reflect his twenty-three years of military service. Michaels enlisted in the Marine Corps in 1970 and has memberships in the Veterans of Foreign Wars, the American Legion, the Disabled American Veterans organizations, NRA, and Rotary International. In 1971, he married his high school sweetheart, raised three daughters and has three grandsons. He calls Creek County, Oklahoma home.

Made in the USA
Columbia, SC
18 February 2019